Meet Aaron, a boy who d [barcode: D0746444]
whose limbs do not support him,
religious cult/sect; Jimmy, his elderly caretaker; and Carly, the homeless vagabond whose violently imagistic inner music washes over us in a hallucinatory rush of the senses. *Light was burning me to a crisp. The floor was all milk.* Everything in Laurie Blauner's magnificent *Out of Which Came Nothing* feels as if it exists in another dimension, a parallel universe where people are flesh and the tangible goods of our world endure but the interior emotional fabric has faded to a monochrome. *I was in a city full of houses that resembled pink and blue bakery boxes and it was snowing outside my window.* Dystopic, perhaps, hyper-realistic, maybe, or most disquieting of all, the real world we inhabit where what *is missing* reflects our essence. A visionary writer like Ernesto Sabato, we enter Blauner's realm through her seer's eye, the velocity of her pacing, and her exquisitely-wrought prose. In this diminished human landscape, the pages mesmerize and turn effortlessly.

Stephanie Dickinson, author of *Razor Wire Wilderness*

With the sure hand of a writer of great power, Laurie Blauner gives us a novel of our time—a novel in which the world has evolved from the real into the suprareal. In this book everything constellates around an idiosyncratic old man named Jimmy and the mysterious adolescent boy, Aaron, he takes care of, who is perhaps avatar, savant, who is blind and cannot talk, and who cannot walk or use his body in normal ways. The precision of Blauner's beautifully executed and deeply imagined prose evokes the sense of dreams that are awake and stronger than reality but are reality. We are presented with the archetypes of our age: the challenged; the world-weary, the homeless, the hallucinators, the would-be saviors manifesting in movements which permeate society and truth, the anxious, the hopeful, the neglected, the lost. Blauner moves us through her novel in linguistic lightning strikes, illuminating and penetrating, but never lingering. *Out of Which Came Nothing* is a stunning book, a book not so much about the change that is coming as the change that has come.

Rosalind Palermo Stevenson, author of *The Absent, Insect Dreams*, and *Kafka at Rudolph Steiner's*

Laurie Blauner's layered characters, drawn with engagingly lyrical language, seem to move patiently in and out of themselves. Every person has a story that has another story within itself. As the world changes, its mysteries grow. The main character, Jimmy, is a retired man with a strong voice, and the disabled boy he cares for (aren't we all disabled in some way?) seems to know more than we realize. Could such a life be made real? Here is a fresh, interesting book about stubborn loneliness and identities in a world where Jimmy transforms, as does THEM, a religion. Kindness and need come down to us together and the thin line between dreams is reality.

Rich Ives, author of *Tunneling to the Moon* and *Light from a Small Brown Bird*

Laurie Blauner's voice is lyrical, her imagery surprising and perfect, her societal observations unbiased. Her attention to detail is stunning, while the broad strokes of the story remain subtle and mysterious. Ghostly memories waft through the pages like fragrances. There is poignancy in the characters inhabiting the pages of this novel. They seem resigned to their brokenness, rarely questioning the forces directing their lives. A gentle, intriguing book about loss and change and the fragility of human connections.

Barbara Lindsay, playwright, author of *The Walkers* and *Possum*

Out of Which Came Nothing

Laurie Blauner

SPUYTEN DUYVIL
NEW YORK CITY

ISBN 978-1-956005-11-0

Library of Congress Cataloging-in-Publication Data

Names: Blauner, Laurie, author.
Title: Out of which came nothing / Laurie Blauner.
Description: New York City : Spuyten Duyvil, [2021] |
Identifiers: LCCN 2021032292 | ISBN 9781956005110 (paperback)
Classification: LCC PS3552.L3935 O98 2021 | DDC 813/.54--dc23
LC record available at https://lccn.loc.gov/2021032292

"Poets claim that we recapture for a moment the self that we were long ago when we enter some house or garden in which we used to live in our youth....It is in ourselves that we should rather seek to find those fixed places, contemporaneous with different years."

In Search of Lost Time by Marcel Proust

"Behold I make all things new."
Revelations 21:5

PART I

CHAPTER ONE, JIMMY

I took care of the boy in my New York City apartment. He wasn't my child. They told me the rules when they gave him to me:

1) you must have clean hands
2) speak clearly, no murmuring
3) keep him unsullied, completely pure in every way
4) someone will come daily to bath him; you can feed him, clean his bed pan, brush and arrange his hair on a pillowcase, etc.
5) move him carefully if you must move him.

The boy was relentlessly pale with fine, black hair. All he could do was blink.

One blink was *yes* and two blinks *no*.

I wanted to ask about what came in between the yes and no but I didn't. I was distracted with my own choices, problems, and memories. I wanted to atone for my life, for what I had done. The boy needed someone and this was my chance to make amends. But to whom? Who was left? Taking care of the boy, Aaron, had initially sounded easy enough.

They told me I wouldn't have to tend him for long because the world I knew was going to end, maybe in a year or two. They said there would be a big stubborn flood like water spilling from an overfilled glass. Or was it fire, raging, hot and devouring, like an insatiable wife? They said I'd see the end only at the very last minute when it would be too late. Or maybe they called it The Change instead of The End. They wouldn't give me details. *Watch*, they said. *It doesn't matter where you go or how high.* My mind argued with them. *Do something,* it whispered. *What about my friends? Couldn't we change anything?*

But I knew they'd only answer about the next life. Perhaps I'd even have a new body, a better one. In the meantime my ancient body grew more afflictions:

1) red, spreading rashes on my limbs

2) stomach aches in waves that crashed against my abdominal skin

3) headaches that simmered between my brain bones

4) and some of my kinky white hair fell out.

I was hoping to be preoccupied with the illnesses to take my mind off of everything else. But the lake of my mind remained as well as the shore that surrounded it. Who could tell the difference?

"Jimmy," they said, the chorus of them, "you must tend Aaron. He's the key to the rest of the world. We're his locks." At least they let me know that much.

"Where's he from?" I stared at his wormy, white fingers, the way his small body fell and tossed around limply when they carried him into the extra room of my apartment.

"Maybe Romania or Russia. We believe he learned English a few years ago, from living here. But not a lot. Didn't you, Aaron?" The man in the suit was standing in front of the child but he hadn't touched the child.

One blink.

"How old is he?"

"Fourteen." A pause. He scratched his head. "We think."

One of the women in a dress smiled, smoothing the new bed sheets. "We know that you'll take good care of him."

I wanted to say that I wasn't sure but nothing came out of my mouth. I hardly knew these people, owed nothing to them or to the boy. "How will I explain him to neighbors, family, or friends?"

"What family?" The man in the suit straightened a photograph near the boy's bed of a forgettable landscape, the standard field, flowers, and trees, that were in the frame when I bought it. He looked around. "What family do you have left, old man? Jimmy, we know that you're good-hearted. Just be careful around friends and neighbors."

"The child, Aaron, is blind and mute and he can't walk," a woman with a flowered apron over her plain dress said plainly. "No one will even know that he's here." She went over to my sink and began to clean the dishes I hadn't used yet.

The man in a suit said, "He's a gift. You're privileged. So please treat him like a precious object." Then they were gone.

I was afraid of the child at first. I tried to ignore him by doing my usual things, reading, watching television, doing crossword puzzles, sitting at my kitchen table, watching the young couple with their new baby across the street. That young woman zigzagged a spoon in the air like a snake preparing to strike before it reached the baby's mouth. Was that something I was going to have to learn to do? Traffic and the noise of the city ebbed and flowed while sunlight consoled me. I lifted my coffee cup to my lips just as someone upstairs shattered something on the floor above my head. I spilled a little. I couldn't hear anything from the child. His silence filled me.

***

The child expanded quickly, his flesh pooling toward the edges of his bed. That was all I did at first, feed the boy. His mouth opened when he heard me and I decided whether to put food or water in it. They told me to feed him whatever I ate. He didn't try to ask for anything. I found myself making more food, trying defiant dishes, spicy spaghetti and meatballs, beef stroganoff for two, or three. I had only cooked for myself for quite a while. Ice cream, chocolate cake, potato chips. Had the boy eaten these before? He gobbled them down. He spit out the spinach.

I was alone. I wasn't alone.

"You have to stop overfeeding him. He won't be ready when the time comes." A woman wearing a bright yellow dress that matched her hair had stopped by to see how he was doing. She checked his bed pan to make sure it was thoroughly clean. Then she used the bed pan to bathe him, splashing water into dark spots on her dress. She had a large nose and large hands that snatched at smaller objects. She used a sponge over his pale, fleshy body and I couldn't look.

I stood at the doorway. "When the time comes for what?" But she didn't answer before she left.

I started questioning the boy when we were alone. "Do you know what they think is going to happen?"

Two blinks. *No.*

"Are you related to any of them?"

The child stared at nothing with his white filmy eyes and long lashes. As if he expected a reply from the walls and ceiling.

"You don't know?"

No answer. He stared.

"My name is Jimmy."

One blink. *Yes.*

"Do you like television?"

Two blinks, then one, then more like Morse Code.

"I have an idea." I found a pencil and paper. I situated them near his soft, grubby fingers but his hands wavered like antennae and couldn't find them. I placed them cross-wise on top of the undershirt sheathing his chest, pulling down the covers. He discovered them.

"Do you know what these are?"

One blink.

"Paper and pencil. Can you write?"

His eyes didn't answer. He continued staring. But his hands became frenzied, touching the paper and pencil, then rearranging them again and again across the expanse of his chest. A brief, preventable smile appeared on his mouth until it hurried away. The white, planetary lump of him humped higher in the bed. Then his unsteady hands began to write as his eyes drifted off toward the floor. He stopped writing. I picked up the piece of paper. I figured that he might like some toys or some special food or fresh air. Or something I hadn't thought of yet. In terrible handwriting scrawled all over the page all it said was *They Very MAD*** to know i hav pen.*

"Why?" I laid the implements on the side of his bed.

Aaron grabbed the pencil and paper and tucked them underneath his pillow. It took all his strength and his muscles quivered like quick, little animals. Then he closed his eyes, lay back down on his bed in the same position I had initially found him in. I was still curious about what was inside of him.

***

This was a typical day for me before the boy came to live with me:

I woke up, lay in bed trying to determine what kind of day it would be from whatever light was visible and from what hurt in my body. Was my pain serious or not? I wondered which muscle or organ would give out just when I needed it most.

Sometimes there was cereal and coffee accompanied by an early tenacious sunlight. I used to work at Grand Central Station with its enormous clock and mannered, elegant architecture. I sold tickets to people hurrying by every day. They were on their way to another life, usually work, which was just like my life, but with less noise, or they were embarking on a vacation or visiting family. All activities I didn't know much about. Then I retired. Lately I go to the nearest subway station just to feel the rush of people on and off the trains. I find their expectations, anticipation, and various emotions and motions soothing. It's a place no one will recognize me or ask me what I'm doing.

Once a man in a dark suit saw me standing by the ticket kiosk. It must have been my posture or dress since he asked me, "Hey, can you tell me where to catch the 510?"

"Nope."

"I thought you worked here. You're here every day at the same time."

Sometimes someone will drop something and I retrieve it for them, following them, calling them, until they're reunited with their personal possession, a baseball, a sequined glove, a scarf with birds on it, a bank receipt, a business report, a seashell in which I could hear the ocean, a plastic spoon. My own life was slowly slipping away from me, so the least I could do was to reunite people with theirs. I was tired of all my experiences. As I chased the people, I could feel pain first in one part of my body and then in another. I was out of breath by the time I reached someone and hardly able to speak. I felt as though something inside of me was waiting to break into tiny little pieces.

Sometimes music echoed down the subway corridors, a band or a single musician asking for money. But it was hard to hear in the tunnel with the rumbling sounds of the trains, conversations, babies crying, children screaming, people's footsteps.

Once an older man, wearing suspenders, jumped in front of a train. But he was coaxed out again quickly by his wife who grabbed him by his shoulders and hoisted him away from the tracks at the right moment.

Most of the time no one noticed that I was there.

When people dressed in black and white first began coming to the subway station I thought they were a family with their matching tee shirts, jackets, and pants. It was a uniform that was hard to ignore. They handed out leaflets that discussed politics and religion, as though the two were always combined. When different people came on different days I began asking questions, to which they often had a short, fast response.

"Who is your leader?" I inquired.

"The great and wondrous Brian," a young man with long, dark hair to his shoulders replied. He held out a dogmatic pamphlet that had the words THEM (Theological Human Evolvement Movement) plastered across the cover with a glossy landscape photograph stuffed full of scenic trees, grass, flowers, and sky.

"Who do you think you're going to find in the subway station?"

"Anyone and everyone." His hair shook as he spoke. He smiled. "I found you." A train squealed by. It was hard to hear him. His eyes appeared too large in the underground fluorescent lights.

"I don't care about politics," I claimed. It was damp down there that day because rain had seeped inside and water was sprinkled all over the cement platform and steps from people's coats, shoes, and umbrellas. My bones shivered.

"Then you must care about religion." He continued passing out his pamphlets. Most people walked by without taking one. "Everyone needs something."

"I've had enough religion." I turned around and left.

But later I did go to a meeting and I found the people there friendly and accommodating enough, although they were vague about their plans and their beliefs. They congregated briefly, confessing the weaknesses in their lives to one another, then they ran off. It felt as though these people were calling to me from a great distance. I didn't feel engaged. But then I wasn't offended either. I must admit being intrigued. After that meeting people in black tee shirts and white pants began appearing everywhere in my life. A hello from an overly friendly shopper at the grocery store. Two women gossiping together on a bus. A red-haired receptionist at my dentist's office. A mother in sneakers and her two children at the library. A girl in her early twenties from a nearby apartment building who dressed as a winged fairy one Halloween, tiptoeing up and down our stairway with some of her friends, trying to look inside keyholes.

"We want a better life," the young man with long hair had said, and I couldn't argue about that. It was what came after life that we could all argue about.

I went to eat lunch with my old friends at a bullet-shaped steel diner where we obliquely discussed some of the things we'd done and our current ideas while silverware winked at us in the inviolable light. Jack had worked in an auto shop,

Don used to work on city roads, and Bill was still trying to manage a stationary store.

"Don't take this the wrong way, fellas," Bill grinned, "but we don't have any family left between the four of us."

"Especially wives," Don said.

"I have half a woman." Jack was eating hash browns. He squeezed ketchup that ricocheted off his plate and came to rest in splotches on the Formica table.

"Is she short, like half a person?" I asked.

"No, just ask her husband." He laughed. "He has one half and I have the other."

"I won't ask which half," Bill cackled.

"Gary, my old boss, is gone now." Don stuffed a hamburger into his mouth, bread and ketchup cascading onto his white plate.

"Everybody seems to be dying," I said.

"He's just retired. He's about ten years younger than I am," Don said, noticeably older.

When the boy came I wanted to tell Jack, Bill, and Don about him. Aaron's care began to take up more of my life. But I was told not to tell anyone.

"Why me for the boy?" I asked a middle-aged woman with her gray hair unraveling from a bun. We were in the bare, simple room before a THEM meeting.

"Because you'll take good care of him." She looked at one of the men. "The rest of us are too busy with our families and work and preparations."

"Preparations for what?" But they wouldn't tell me. I

wasn't part of their core group, the true believers who unquestioningly did everything that was requested of them.

"It's an honor to take care of him. Aaron is special. You're chosen, Jimmy." The woman looked at a man who was setting up more folding chairs in the rectangular room. People were starting to file in. "He'll fill up your life."

Did I have to believe in the boy? Did I believe that Aaron could ever do anything more than learn to feed himself one day?

"Your mind seems to be elsewhere. Where did you go, Jimmy?" Don had finished eating.

"I'm here." I continued eating my cheese sandwich, my mind sliding to a halt.

"Glad you're back," Bill said.

"Is there something you want to tell us?" Jack laughed good-naturedly.

"No," I said. "Absolutely not."

The rest of my afternoon and evening I usually spent watching the furiously lit television or reading. I had just begun some books about transparent fish, mutations newly discovered in the ocean. Next I wanted to read about inventions. Last Halloween a small vampire, whom I heard gliding up and down the stairs, sometimes unsuccessfully, knocked at my door.

"You're the only tenant who's opened their door." She straightened up in her wobbly, black high heels, tight black pants, some sort of shawl, and sunglasses. She was a young girl, who was taller than she appeared through my peep-hole.

"Maybe the others just expected you to pass right through their doors as if the wood hardly existed." I went to rummage up some old candy and pennies.

I often spied on neighbors in the hallway through my peephole, especially when the couple at the end of the floor were fighting outside their front door. Some days I tried to predict who was traveling up and down the stairs by the sound of their shoes or their voices or their humming. It must be how the boy felt about the noise in the world around him. I had learned in a recent book that bats detected their environment by the quality of sound that bounced off of unaccustomed objects. The girl was waiting at the door with her sunglasses perched on her nose and her blue eyes curious about anything she could see inside my apartment. I handed her some old Tootsie rolls and spare change.

"Don't you have anything better, like Reese's or Mounds bars or chocolates or something?"

"How old are you?"

"Sixteen."

"Isn't that a little too old to be Trick or Treating?"

"I was bored. Don't you like my costume?" She twirled around on her toes, smiling and showing her fangs, which resembled the cheap plastic fork prongs used for deli food, until she almost became a black blur. Her eyes seemed to glow in the dimly lit hallway. They flashed with yellow flecks and focused on me. "What's your name?"

"Jimmy."

"My name's Emily and my mother's the whore on the third floor." She pointed upstairs and awkwardly pursed her lips over her plastic inserts. "She told me to go out and play." She smiled unevenly. "So that's what I'm doing."

My days flew by and at night I was restless. One early November night I dreamt of a black-haired girl who looked like Emily (thin nose, big ears, awkward arms and legs). But she was older and dressed in white as a nurse. Her arms flew around my kitchen.

"Every creature knows when it's loved," she cried. "I need to find an antidote for the wrong kind of love." She held her face in her fists.

Then she peered at me. "Or else we both need to learn how to make better choices."

Suddenly she was searching through papers in my table drawers. "The right equation is everything or nothing." She looked at me innocently, begging for a remedy. Her need hung in the air between us, puffing then collapsing my kitchen curtains.

Chapter Two, Jimmy

"Maybe we're not as profound as we think," a woman with gray braids and a copper bracelet exclaimed. She wanted to direct my life.

I was at a meeting, surrounded by proselytizing people who wore the usual black and white clothes. Sometimes they wore the shirt and pants beneath their coats or street clothes to remind themselves who they really were. There were young, old, black, white, brown, thin, fat, brunettes, blondes, redheads, the rich, and poor.

"Brian is just a man," I offered, "but with a very large boat." They believed in goodness and something else that wasn't articulated, something they thought might happen. For them death held so many possibilities.

"He's working hard." Her braids whirled around, in their own private world. "I just meant for today. We don't seem to be finding a way to reach more people." Her eyes widened. "I heard you've got Aaron."

"My apartment's pretty empty. That's probably why they gave me the boy."

"There were other reasons."

I wanted to ask her more but the singing began. Songs rose toward the bright lights as if they knew exactly where they were going. Introductions were made all around and a discussion of philosophies and deeds ensued while my legs began to swell. One person claimed he could see the dead. The dead told him all kinds of things like how to fix broken cars or how to bake an upside down cake or how an encaustic painting looked like something underwater. The sky at the windows was dank-looking, waiting also for something illuminating. I told the woman with gray braids about my absent beliefs. We were both drinking coffee and she mumbled some reply.

"Are you planning something I need to know about?" My coffee scalded my lips. The cookies were leaden and tasted too sweet under the fluorescent lights.

She shook her head.

I needed to confess that the boy was gummy, white, and spreading. He made me uncomfortable. There was some part of myself that I hated and that part had become the boy. Yet he was growing. In the last two weeks he'd already outgrown the shirts and pants he had arrived in.

"Doesn't he need to see a doctor sometime?"

"I don't know. Whatever the governing group told you." The woman, Rosemary, whisked her braids to one shoulder and pulled at them while people greeted one another all around us. "I remember my mother asking last week, 'Where's my son? Where's my darling son?' But she only has a daughter, me. What can you say to that kind of question?"

"Yes," I said, "most questions can get up and walk around on their own."

"Or ask themselves," she grinned.

"Now if they could only answer themselves we could start a whole new religion." I enjoyed teasing her.

"Perhaps someday we'll be worshipping you." She smiled and her lips cracked.

***

That night I was staring at the thin, white, empty walls of my rented living room, my questions leaned against a few dark shadows that I called my furniture. I'd grown used to their patient animal shapes. Behind the walls I imagined other lives springing up and cart-wheeling all around Aaron and me, flinging their problems against the walls in their own apartments. The two of us were marooned in my apartment, unmoving, unspeaking, uncomfortably uncertain of one another.

I turned on the light in the boy's room, illuminating a bed, a chair, and a dresser. The boy's eyelids rolled open, showing a filmy, white layer. His hands stirred, circling his sheets. I noticed black dots along a wrist beneath his shirt. I lifted his hand to inspect it but he pulled it away. He blinked, made murmuring sounds. I reached under his pillow and retrieved the pen. I found his paper and it said: *enuf is enuf.*

His flesh was quivering, his hands covered his eyes, tears squeezed out through his fingers. He hardly made a sound.

"I'm going to wash you," I told him, knowing I could hardly carry him. I awkwardly carried him into the bathtub with a heavy thump and removed his clothes. His body disgusted me. I ran the water. The marks along his left arm and over his heart hadn't bled much and would heal. They resembled a row of ants marching along his limbs. As the water drained away he stopped whimpering. He blinked *no* over and over again.

"What?" My arms grew tired as I dried him and dressed him. I stopped myself from flinching when I touched his soft skin. "You're just a boy." I haltingly carried him back to his bed. I hesitated before I gave him back his pen and paper.

"Where were you before being here?"

He wrote: *mother wi Hard Hand, tech me to write, many kid. THEY buy me. TV?*

"You want to listen to the TV?"

Lots of blinks. I took the pen and paper away.

I thought, *why not?* I knew they wouldn't like it. Aaron reminded me of the woman I'd seen in the subway in torn clothes who begged sometimes. She said crazy things. She was eating from the trash and people ignored her. One day she disappeared. Then the next week she was back. "Where did you go?" I asked her once.

"Hibernation," she spit over her shoulder. She held up an empty snow globe, shaking it. "You know, one of them places without gravity."

I set up the small television in Aaron's room and my arms were already sore from all that lifting. The news was on and the newscasters were saying something about caring for the homeless and then about a plane that had crashed in a foreign country. It was late and I fell asleep on my couch, listening to a man reciting the day's events from the boy's room.

The next morning his left ear was bleeding onto his

pillow in apologetic drips. The television was still talking. "Your ear's bleeding." Most of his pen marks had faded while two had become welts.

His hand flew to his ear and blood gloved his fingers. I swabbed his ear and his fingers and called the phone number I'd been given.

A man answered and when I told him the problem he said, "I'll send someone over immediately."

"Good. We're not going anywhere."

"You're keeping him pure?" he asked.

"Sure." I must have sounded tentative.

"You know he can't have any contact with the outside world." Then the man hung up.

***

The man who knocked at my door was close to my age, wider, wore a black suit, a white shirt, thin eyeglasses. His white hair was shorn nearly down to his scalp, whereas my wild hair whisked kitchen cabinets when I turned too quickly. He carried a small, dark cloth bag. After I opened the door and the man had entered I noticed Emily fidgeting on the landing, near the steps.

"What's going on, Jimmy? An emergency? I've helped my mother with lots of emergencies." She tried to sound wise as she hopped from bare foot to bare foot in her pink shorts and silver tube top. I held my breath for a moment and my heart clenched at the unexpected sight of her. She moved out of the dimly lit hall toward my door. She poked her head inside my apartment, after the man had entered and was standing inside. "Hmm, this is nicer than ours. Or maybe it's just emptier."

"No, Emily, it's not an emergency." I tried to sound soothing. "It's just something in my chest and shoulders that has been bothering me." I had to gently push her back outside my door. Young people were so flagrant with their bodies. Mine had scars from an old, forgotten war, a childhood fall from a bicycle, and a heart operation. It was hard to maintain the body's equilibrium.

"I want to know what you're hiding inside there, Jimmy." She smiled, impishly.

I closed and locked the door.

The man nodded at me. "Where's the boy?" he asked mechanically. I pointed toward my extra room and the man went in without knocking.

I thought about all the worlds that were currently colliding. The boy's limited one, my elderly, fading one, Emily's curious, lively one, and THEM, focused and otherworldly. I stretched my neck and arms and heard my bones cracking. Some days everything hurt and doing any little task took too long. Today the weather paused, and light hadn't begun its luminescent race yet. I watched clouds move behind buildings, trying to hide themselves. The city was self-sufficient, as if it was all that existed.

I'd heard the names of other cities when I worked at Grand Central, but they were far away. I didn't know them or see them. I'd never been outside of my own city. I made up imaginary places, one city where no one was allowed to get married or have children, single people roaming into each other. One in which everything had to be blue (blue buildings, streets, cars, clothes, tableware), and one where it rained so much it became an underwater city with people swimming to their destinations, all their furniture floated.

People departed and arrived from the cities in my job but the places were never real to me. They were only names, Boston, Philadelphia, Chicago, Passaic, or New Haven, which sounded refreshing. I thought of a city, called West Woods, that had buildings painted all kinds of pale colors and a forest that circled it. I wasn't sure whether it actually existed or not. Maybe I had overheard someone talking about it.

The man emerged from the bathroom. His hands appeared to be struggling with one of my towels. He looked around. "Have you ever had a family?"

"No." But I was betraying Martine and Phillip who visited me illicitly between sleep and waking.

"Well, then I'll explain what you need to do." He launched into details about creams, bandages, and pills and about moving him so he wouldn't get bed sores. "I'll let THEM know and they can check on the progress of his healing."

"Fine." I showed him out the door. I noticed two bare feet scurrying upstairs in the hallway just outside my apartment.

I went into the boy's room. "I'm sorry. I guess I shouldn't have brought you the television." He didn't move. He was on his back, as usual, with his eyes closed, covers near his neck. He was his own world. Maybe he was asleep. I couldn't tell.

That night, before bed, I mumbled a few beseeching words and threw them toward the indeterminate sky. I prayed that Emily hadn't heard anything.

***

The next morning I went in to see the boy and change his bandage. The doctor gave me a pamphlet they recommended that I read to Aaron. I began:

"*At first everything was left to itself, to grow unfettered, to play or run wild. Animals and people understood one another and cooperated. Then a man came to show the world what more it could be. There were so many versions that people had to decide for themselves which way they wanted to go. His name was Brian. One of Brian's sons lived in every city and they all grew up to be politicians except for one. He didn't really grow up at all. He was poor, ragged, and shy and kept to himself. Because he couldn't walk or talk or see, he begged on the streets of a big city where people passed him by every day. Some people pushed him out of their way or spit at him, beat him or robbed him of the little money he had.* He began to say things like, 'A mouth and eyes inside of me tell me what to do.' 'When we are gone we will be replaced.' 'Something from my body wants the rest of the world.' *People began to listen.*

This son grew older, sadder, and stronger. He talked about how the mind was a network of bees and how we were all in-

terrelated. *When this son ran for an important government position he won. Brian died and this special son took his place. All the people and the animals began to rely on this son for guidance. What is this needy disease? he asked. The animals grew frightened and ran away. Anger rose up in the son and nothing could extinguish it, not his new wife or sons, not gifts from the people or the whole world lying, shaky, at his feet. The son felt nothing was worthy so he wanted a whole new world..."*

I stopped reading and looked at the boy. He didn't look different. There was no expression on his pale, puffy face. I gave him the pen and paper.

Don Under stand.

"We'll read other things. I have some very good books here."

WAN See Girl otside.

"You know about her? Emily?" I was surprised.

Cann hear.

"Maybe next time I see her."

Cann hear in Her Room. Cann hear she lonely. The boy sat up in his bed and moved his useless legs like logs not connected to his body underneath his blanket.

"Would you like some food? They'll be here soon."

Too day am 15.

"Happy Birthday then." How would he know? Did he mean it? Was he keeping track of the days?

There was a knock at the door and Rosemary, the woman with gray braids, entered with another younger woman in a white dress.

"Hello Jimmy." She threw her stubborn braids to the

back of her plaid shirt and they rested there. "Where's Aaron?"

I pointed at the extra room and the woman in white went in there. She left the door ajar. I heard a slight thump on the floor and then her soft, mumbling prayers.

"Would you like some coffee?" I asked Rosemary. I could see inside the room and the woman in white was down on her knees at the side of the boy's bed. Her hands were clasped and the boy had his pale, chubby fingers on top of hers. I was embarrassed, like a witness to a crime.

Rosemary shook her head. "I'm glad you took the boy." She placed a hand with blue, ropey veins and speckled age spots on top of my gnarled, useless one. "You're kind. I can tell from your eyes." She stared into my eyes. "The meek shall inherit the earth." She removed her hand and opened the boy's door, walked inside, leaving the door pushed aside. The other woman didn't turn or look in her direction as she entered. Rosemary kneeled slowly and also began praying aloud. I couldn't hear the two women but I could see their lips moving. Insubstantial murmuring swirled around them.

Something rose up in me between anger, disgust, jealousy, and a sadness over wasted efforts. I didn't want to watch them tend to him so I decided to meet Don, Jack, and Bill, my friends, for lunch after going to the subway station. I grabbed my wallet.

As I turned the knob on the front door the woman in the white dress asked me loudly from the boy's room, "So, Jimmy, who is Emily?"

I ran out the door.

***

At a subway station, farther away from my apartment than usual, I began to notice the disabled. I watched to see how people treated them and to see how they coped. A man without a leg was on crutches, a boy missing his arms used his torso to push open the doors, blind people tapped canes all around, and an older, blue-haired woman was being pushed in a wheelchair. Of course there were people whose problems weren't readily apparent like the boy who couldn't stop laughing or the man terrified of the war that happened continuously, surrounding him. The man who was having an animated conversation with a bench about giraffes or the woman wearing two coats pushing around a grocery cart who screamed every time a train went by. Were the people at THEM cultivating the boy's disabilities to take advantage of him or to make him better? Was the boy capable of lying?

I sat on a bench for a while feeling the spasmodic rush of people. It was life, accelerated. I usually noticed the odd things, a little girl picking her doll's nose, a well-dressed man petting his small dog and then his own face, and a teenage boy with notes taped onto his shoes dancing. I liked seeing that. It was contagious.

But this time I noticed leg braces, mechanical arms, voice boxes, even elevated shoes, devices that fulfilled our wishes. Devices that helped us become our better selves.

A man came up to me. He wore blue jeans and a torn

tee shirt. He shook terribly as he began to speak, "What are you looking at, Mister?"

"I was thinking about where the body ends and the mind begins," I answered.

He was surprised for a moment. Then he pointed at himself, "Parkinson's." He smiled. "But I tell little kids that I was standing too close to a passing train, and now I'm this way."

"I have a child that's different."

"Yeah," he said, "do you have a cigarette?"

"No."

"Have you found Jesus?"

"Yes," I said. "And I'm going to return him."

***

Bill, Jack, and Don were already eating inside the diner, filled with a syrupy light. Clouds tumbled and air flailed at people's jackets outside our window. Mustard had spilled and was streaked across the table and on napkins. A generalized music played softly from hidden speakers from the corners of the restaurant. The linoleum floor gleamed.

"Glad you could make it, Jimmy," Don said, dipping a French Fry into ketchup and tossing it into his mouth.

"Do you think that the deepest part of the soul is dark?" I asked.

"Whoa," Jack said, "that's a heavy question."

"I'm Catholic," Bill piped up.

"I don't mean anything about religion," I said.

"Oh," Bill said and all three of them continued eating.

I ordered a ham sandwich.

"With some nothingness on the side," Jack laughed.

"Something's going on with you, Jimmy, and someday I'm sure you'll tell us what it is. How long have we known one another?" Don inquired. A splotch of ketchup stained his chin.

"Twenty-seven years," Bill answered.

"Maybe more," Jack said. "Thirty."

Don flipped some nonexistent hair from his forehead, returned from his thoughts and said, "No, I think there's a little bit of light in even the darkest part of the soul. But there couldn't be light without darkness."

"That's pretty noncommittal," I answered.

"It takes one to know one," Bill said.

"I wish I could go deeper," I said, wanting to get to the unseen, past all the surfaces.

"Count me out," Jack grinned amiably. Don and Bill nodded in agreement.

***

"Here's another story they wanted me to read to you." I picked up the same pamphlet they had given me before and pretended to read from it, turning the pages.

The boy looked disappointed, his features sagging toward his doughy face, as though someone might hit him.

"A boy that understood himself was born but he couldn't escape his body. He wondered about green grass, the sky, rain.

He slept many days and nights because he was left to himself.
He tried to discover how to make all the things outside him be-
come a part of him, subway trains, television, ice cream." But I
hadn't thought any farther.

The boy blinked once. He wrote *do i owe Them?*

I sighed, closed the booklet, rubbed my sore knees. Was
he a punishment? For what? For losing Phillip and Martine? I began his morning rituals, bed pan, brushing his
teeth and his agitated hair. Even I, Jimmy Hatfield, wanted
to be part of something bigger than myself, old and argumentative as I was.

***

Rosemary, with her gray, unruly braids, came with another woman who put on an apron so she wouldn't soil her
lacy dress. "It's such a privilege to take care of the boy. I enjoy taking care of people myself. Hey, I didn't see you come
to a meeting last week," Rosemary said.

"I was busy," I said.

"We need to know how the boy's doing."

"Fine, as usual."

"Especially after the ear incident."

So they had heard about that. I sat down wearily, some
of my bones creaking. A rash I had was subsiding. "Maybe
I'm not the person for this job." I knew how secrets told
themselves. It was only a matter of time. I'd lived long
enough to know that.

"We'll help you as much as you'd like. Is there anything
I can do for you now?"

"You can show me what you both do to clean him. Then you only need to come in the afternoons."

"Okay," Rosemary was standing. "But are you sure you want to be responsible for all that? We know about what happened with Martine."

"That was a long time ago." It was a previous life. "Yes, I want to try." This was my new life.

***

I had one of my excruciating headaches and then I was dreaming. I was in a city full of houses that resembled pink and blue bakery boxes and it was snowing outside my window. Frosting covered everything. The boy was tall, thinner, with a fringe of black hair on his head and the dusting of a moustache below his nose. He was now a man. He entered a pale green room which, except for the color, was exactly like my bedroom.

"I see you're feeling better." Aaron bent down, expertly held my wrist between his fingers, calculating my pulse.

"Aaron?"

"Who else could it be?" He stood and an easy laugh flew from his throat.

"How can you be walking and talking?"

He sat back down again. "Hmm, maybe you're not better after all." He frowned, stared at me.

"And your eyes!" I drew a line in the air and his eyes followed it. "How did you get better? When did you grow up?"

"Jimmy, you DO need my help, don't you?" Aaron

laughed again, a melodious sound that rang against the walls of my bedroom. "I've been grown for a while."

I sat up, disheveling my sheets and blanket. But my head throbbed so insistently I had to lie back down. "What are you doing now?" I noticed some of my hair left on my pillow.

"Taking care of you for one thing."

"Who's taking care of you while I have this headache?" I held the top of my head where it hurt.

Aaron laughed. "No one. I don't need anything, which is more than I can say for you, old man."

"Tell me more about yourself. What do you do every day?"

"I take care of lost, broken children." He patted my hand. "That's how I grew up. That's how I healed. But you already knew that." He smiled his dazzling, unencumbered smile. "I know what you're really asking." He walked to the door of my bedroom and opened it.

Aaron's later selves marched through the room. First a man in his late youth with a black beard and moustache, slim yet energetic. Then a middle-aged man, clean-shaven, with thinning, peppery hair and wrinkles forming around his eyes and mouth. Lastly an old man, nearly my age, with spots of white hair, creases lined his face, and his flesh seemed to drip from his bones. He moved slowly.

I shook the bony hand of the oldest Aaron who inched toward me. I was going to ask him an important question. Then I woke up.

Thirty years ago I had noticed Martine and her son, Phillip, on a bench at Grand Central Station. She was brushing his tufted hair with the palm of her hand on a Monday morning. By Monday afternoon he was playing with a paper airplane on top of a large, rectangular piece of luggage. Tuesday morning Martine, with her dark hair pulled back, her ebony skin, was eating an orange. Tuesday afternoon she was reading a book by Proust in French. She propped it against her bag while Phillip, a tiny, black boy of nine, ran around her bench in circles. I said hello inquisitively as I passed them and she said hello back warily. Wednesday I offered her half of my tuna sandwich, which she accepted. I was an older white man in a uniform. I sat down.

"Are you waiting for someone?"

"No." Her English was broken. She was nervous.

"Are you going somewhere?"

"Someday." Tears surfaced in her eyes. "So many people they coming and going. Nobody see us here."

The boy stopped playing and sat on the other side of her. He stared at a very young girl, holding hands with her mother. She walked past him with a small brown bag in her other hand. Phillip leaned his curly head onto his mother's lap. She gave him most of the tuna sandwich. "You can stay here as long as you want, but this isn't a good place to sleep in."

"It be fine."

Thursday I brought four sandwiches, sardine, tuna, cheese, and ham, which disappeared quickly. Martine's dark hair was in greasy clumps against her head and Phillip's smelled of the soap from the men's room. "Do you have any money?"

"No," Martine shook her head tearfully. "We run away from new husband bad to us." She watched her boy chasing a withered red balloon. "I get married so I stay and what happen? Martine need to go, but I no go back to islands."

"You and the boy could come and stay with me tonight if you want. I've got an extra room. I could use the company." I took a handkerchief out of my pocket and offered it to her but she shook her head. "I'll come by and get you when I'm done with work."

She smiled shyly. Martine.

"All objects are extensions of the body." I wasn't sure Aaron would understand what I meant. I had rented a collapsible wheelchair and had it delivered. The boy's body was heavier than I remembered. I lifted him. My legs and arms shook as I ladled him into the blue slung seat. I almost dropped him. "Are you okay with this?"

One blink. *Yes.*

I wheeled him around the apartment. He smiled and reached his hands out for what was invisible to him when we stopped near furniture. He blinked and blinked but I couldn't tell what he was trying to say. Every few minutes his hands whirred in excitement.

I opened a window, and a mild October sky, dirt, traffic noise, light, and broken dreams rushed in. He closed his eyes and looked almost normal. I was a shadow behind him. We moved in small circles and figure eights around my sofa, tables, and chairs. The wheels squeaked and my legs groaned, but then the boy touched the wheels and helped roll himself into the furniture. He tried to push out his hands when he bumped into things, but it was already too late.

I finally realized that he wanted the pen and paper.

I stand.

"No," I told him, "my arms aren't strong enough. And THEM would be angry." I wondered, for the first time, if I was holding him back. I wheeled him into the bedroom and shoveled him into the bed. I hoped no other part of him would bleed. I didn't know about the boy, but I was exhausted. My world was small but not as small as the boy's. We both needed more world.

***

That evening there was a knock at the door. Emily was twitching and shuffling from bare foot to bare foot. She wore a tight, red dress with a v down the front and a little of her spilled out of it.

"Did your shoes escape?"

"I heard some weird sounds coming from your apartment today." She stopped fidgeting and stared at me. Her eyes were an anxious blue color like they needed to leave soon.

"Like what?"

"Like you were riding a bicycle or roller skating."

"I'm tired, Emily. Would you like to come inside?"

"Yeah."

"You're upstairs from me and you heard all that?"

"Yeah."

The world was at my door and I had just invited it in-side. She must have been trying to listen.

I left the repeating television on and Emily walked to my sofa and made herself at home. She casually looked around my living room. There was a large mouth on the television screen that slipped a pill inside its lips. The mouth said something about "never being sad again."

"Do you have any shoes?" I asked her soft feet.

"Yes, Jimmy," she sighed. "Of course I have shoes. I have lots of cute shoes." She smiled. "But sometimes I like sneak-ing around so people can't hear me."

"What have you learned from that?"

She looked at the crevices in my ceiling. "That the apart-ment next to us has two families living there with tons of kids. And the people down the hall on this floor, to the left of you, like to choke each other during sex. And some guy at the far end plays the tuba when he hopes nobody's at home. There's a woman who makes paper dolls one floor above us. Why? What do you want to know, Jimmy?"

"I don't know. Facts." She couldn't tell me what I wanted to know, which was what lay between awareness and un-consciousness underneath someone else's skin. That place where we were each stunned by our own ideas, forgotten secrets, and dreams. Did we hope that someone or some-thing else had all our answers?

"Those can be hard to find." She nodded. "Facts about

what? What people do? Then you still need more facts to figure out why they do it." She crossed her legs and one was beating up and down nervously.

"Every story is a little bit of a horror story," I began, preparing her to meet the boy. I had considered asking her to help me take the boy outside someday but I decided not to tell her about him. THEM wouldn't like it. "You must have heard me moving furniture around. It was just the whim of an old man."

"It sounded more like a machine."

"Maybe you heard something from the television." I stood up. "I need to do other things right now, Emily. Time for you to go."

She stood and went to the door. She smiled. "You're not fooling me, Jimmy."

I watched Emily's red back scurry up a floor, her bare feet pounded the stairs.

I heard her mother scream, "Emily, is that you? I need some dinner. I'm hungry now."

I thought of Emily's legs churning past her mother, hurrying further and further away from her. Until Emily could finally look backward and see a woman who could never be satisfied or healthy. And by that time Emily would be long gone.

***

I tidied up the kitchen and then sat down on the wheezing sofa. The boy was too quiet. Sometimes he made a low moaning sound that reminded me of frightened animals. I looked out my window, saw an airplane repositioning itself behind a brick building. A ghostly face appeared and then disappeared at an apartment across the alley. I knew the world would continue no matter what I did to it. I missed the hum of people's lives, the frenzied time, the way some of us intersected at train stations. The dead sky of memory was at the window. Sometimes the city helped a wizened elderly man with white hair, and other times I had to reject help because it cost too much. I picked up Stephen Hawking's *The Brief History of Time,* imagining a city in which time didn't exist in the normal sense. Someplace where a person could go backwards or forwards in time at will, which was confusing for the people around that person.

I was thinking how I had always done what I was told. Out of which came nothing. I began daydreaming about taking the boy out with Emily. Then my head fell onto my chest and the book slipped out of my hands.

Chapter Three, Carly

"Everything's inside my body," I screamed, pulling strands of my long, greasy hair out from under a hat. "Everything that's supposed to be outside my body is inside," I finished telling anyone who would listen. It was important. It made sense. I wanted everyone to know it could happen to them.

I gathered my rags around my chest, pulled my hat down on my head that kept sparks from train wheels away from the paper wadded in my brain. They could hurt me. So many things had hurt me, cats, whirring machines, stuff from the sky, boxes with eyes, the color blue.

Once I caught a man's briefcase reaching out toward me, and he was the one that started shouting for the police. I tried to press charges, but no one listened to me. I still needed to tell them how names were pianos without legs and they tasted like eggs in your mouth. I won't tell anyone my name, not even the police when they've asked politely. "I like it down here," I've told them again and again when they wanted to move me. All I wanted to do was to explain and to keep pushing my cart that held everything that fell into my body, a green wig, a dress for birds, a dead spider, a box of coat hangers, a zoo coin stamped with trees.

Then I was talking to a group of Disables. The old man had whirlwind white hair, which was a good sign, and he was wheeling a pale boy with dark hair who gurgled at everything. There was a young girl in red trailing behind them, taking notes, and her blue eyes burned through me. I knew she could hurt me. She looked away as a train came, filling up the tunnel with noise. That was my chance.

I yelled at them, "My doubt is lost without me." The weird boy's head snapped toward me, but his eyes were poisoned, probably from bad dreams. His soft, fat hands flew into the air. His spine and legs were caught in a machine that went places. He was young. The old man gave him a pen and paper.

He wrote *Tell her maybe Death or something like it will come. Maybe a push against the floor. But not singing. Singing won't happen.*

The old man showed me the note and said, "He never wrote anything like that to me." He looked more closely. "I wonder what he means."

"Means, means. By all means." The boy was the only person listening to me. I had to warn him about dark glasses, collapsed windows, smears of blue on doors, and so many other things I couldn't list them all. The boy's head nodded as if he understood. The trains were gone. I waited first, then explained, "I feed them fallen pigeons so they won't come after me."

"Are you going somewhere?" the old man asked. "Here." He held out a palm with two dollars on it.

I snatched the money away. I knew he was good luck. "I've seen you here before," I said.

The old man nodded. "My name's Jimmy."

"Mine's Natasha." I was putting on airs. I held out a gloved hand but a chunk of the glove fell off. I hid it in my basket but I could feel that piece of glove inside me. Right near my hip. I held my stomach. "Everything hurts," I confessed.

"I know."

"Is that Thing with you?" I pointed at the young girl near the Lost and Found, my favorite place. She looked like something that would come out at night, her eyes very blue.

"Who?"

By the time he looked she was gone. Good, because I thought she wanted to sap my strength. I pointed to where she faded into the walls. Another piece of my glove fell off into my liver.

Then the boy got excited but there weren't any words there.

The old man wheeled the boy near a bench and sat, watching the trains as if he was waiting for introductions.

"I don't want that dirty Thing with its fingers coming back," I yelled at them.

"Don't worry," the old man said. He sighed.

The boy wrote *Even tigers and lions tell shadows their names. This is the start of something, you and me.*

"He's never that eloquent. His spelling has improved."

I breathed in his note and it became my lung. I was starting to like the boy even more. Then the old man looked around and wheeled the boy toward a train with its jaws open. Things were streaming in and out. I looked for the girl but I couldn't see her. They got inside all that metal. It told me more than I wanted to know so I couldn't enter one anymore. Then it whisks people somewhere. Everyone makes believe they know where they're going. The old man strapped the boy and his machine to a seat. The doors were closing. Then the old man, Jimmy, ran out. The doors closed behind him. His breath thumped as he sat and stared at the train becoming a dot of light down the tunnel.

I started to scream at him, "I know what you're doing." I threw words at him, then a clock and a door knob from my cart.

The old man started to cry. "That's good because I don't."

I patted him as if he was a lacy white dress, a little at a time.

Chapter Four, Jimmy

I never understood my relationship to children. They fascinated and scared me. They had a separate world with its own language, gestures, and meanings that paralleled our adult world. Sometimes children were within our world but most of the time, they didn't want anything to do with it. Eventually the children, too, would try to comprehend this adult world that they had inherited. Sometimes they had to change it.

I checked on the boy who hadn't moved an inch all night long. His eyes were closed, his blanket tucked tightly at his chin. I couldn't tell if he was sleeping. The beginning of each new day stunned me toward a cup of coffee. I was glad to be alive.

I was fascinated by his spasmodic throat when he ate or drank. I watched his features collecting information, his head rotating at some new sound. I wanted to pet him sometimes but I was afraid he'd bite me. He was new and different and I didn't know what was inside of him. I could still think of him as filled with anyone or anything I desired. He wasn't himself yet. I was too old and unsteady to move him down my hallway stairs by myself. But every boy needed pleasures and challenges to grow and survive.

Phillip and Martine had gone outside my apartment tentatively at first, as though someone would catch them and return them to the islands, or to the giant hand of her husband, who would sweep them up and squeeze them into nothing. I gave them a quick tour of my drab neighborhood, where everything seemed to be the color of ash. By the third week Phillip went outside by himself with Martine trying to watch him from supervisory windows.

One day Phillip met some adolescent boys, who lured him out of the alley with a game of baseball. In the nearby park they began to tease him about his homemade clothes, his threadbare shoes. Some of the kids, including the black ones, told him his skin was too black and he was too small. Phillip wasn't used to this kind of cruelty although he already knew familial and political cruelty. It surprised him. He said that he cried noisily when they threw balls at him, hitting his arms and legs. He tried to hide and they laughed uncontrollably, doubling over, snickering.

Phillip lifted up his arms and claimed, "I can't help the way I look." He ran behind some arterial trees.

"Look at that piece of shit run. He's faster than I thought. Maybe we should let him on our team," one of the boys said, joking with the others.

Phillip didn't remember picking up one of the bats and smashing an older boy in the knees, but he remembered hearing a crack. He said the boy fell, making the sound of breaking sticks. Then the other boys came toward him from some trees with a look on their faces that reminded him of his mother. He described the feeling of a door suddenly open. Then he could see what he had done.

Cruelty was everywhere I looked, people snapping at one another for all kinds of reasons. The way we bargained

with each other to try and get what we thought we deserved. Were animals cruel when they ate other animals?
You never knew what would emerge from someone.

At THEM meetings my tongue rattled around in my
mouth, holding back my words. I didn't understand some
of the punishments, fire, water, sacrificing your children,
your family. Interpretations were difficult, arbitrary, worse
than in the novels I read. Except for *Crime and Punishment*
or *Tess of the D'Urbervilles* God's voice was described as an
echo down a subway tunnel that burned everything. Sometimes we were cruel to each other without knowing it.

One night I told Martine and Phillip I would take them
out for a special dinner to celebrate our being together. Martine, with her beautiful, loose, black shining hair. I wanted to go to a restaurant where mirrors multiplied people,
where women my age clustered in dresses and gloves for
special occasions, eating on linen tablecloths. I wanted to
show Martine off, see how we all looked together, reflected,
a tentative family. But I knew Phillip would be bored. We
went to Chevy's Cheese instead, where children ran past
cheese fountains, cheese houses, cheese games. Light was
flung around, and the children's families huddled at brightly colored tables. Food was called Big Cheese, Swiss Family
Steak, Cheddar Head Sandwich.

I had to shout at Martine over the cartoon music. "Is
there anything else you want, Martine?"

"You good to us, Jimmy." She was watching Phillip moving in a current of children scurrying around the room trying to touch everything.

"You know you both can stay. I like having you at my apartment."

"I find job."

"You don't have to. I work." I wanted to keep her all for myself.

"Phillip in school. I work." Her hair lashed her cheeks. She wouldn't look at me.

"Is this a dream? I like being with you," I said, reaching for her hand, one finger separated by her wedding band, resting on the shockingly yellow table. "Both."

"I married, Jimmy. You know."

"We can fix that."

But she tore away from me, crying. She grabbed Phillip's small hand and broke him away from the chain of the other children. She ran out of the restaurant sobbing.

"Why is the end of the world so dramatic? Can't it end with a whimper?" I never minded a good argument.

Rosemary's gray braids pinwheeled around her body, hitting her ample chest and her back. "That's how it's told." She was digging in her large bag full of wipes and ointments and other things for Aaron. I could see that I was annoying her. She was trying to ignore me.

"Why bother to do anything then?"

"This world will fold into the next. Who's to say that we'll even notice the difference?" Her hands were rummaging for some article in her bag.

"Maybe it already has."

"Maybe," she barked, visibly irritated. "Alright." She

sighed heavily and stopped her search and looked at me. She sat, defeated-looking, on my deflating sofa.

"Are questions so bad?" I could see wrinkles pinching her eyes and between her nose and mouth.

"Faith is knowing that it will all turn out okay, no matter what."

"Trains don't run on faith. What do you know about the boy?"

"I heard rumors that he was bought at an orphanage from an Eastern Bloc country. I know he's lived in some of our houses, and it hasn't worked out, because there were too many other kids, too much work. I had him for a short time, but I have to help my dying mother." She turned away, her hand thrust back into her jiggling bag. I was trying to take away something from her, just like with Martine, something that was hers alone.

"If I did something wrong with Aaron would he be taken away?" I wasn't done with him yet. I wanted to do something right with the boy.

"Maybe."

"I've already messed up." More than once.

"Why? Are you thinking about stealing him? Or are you trying to get rid of him?"

"Neither. Both," I answered. "I'm going out." But, as usual, I had no idea about where I was going.

***

I didn't have far to go to Grand Central Station from my apartment but I counted the steps, seventy-eight with several curbs. There were overflowing garbage cans, scribbled and shattered bus stop shelters, hydrants, streetlights, and signs. A girl sat on the sidewalk outside of the station, cross-legged with a guitar on her knees. She wore sunglasses and a hat of gnats circled her although it was almost winter. Her silver jewelry clacked as she strummed.

"Memories are all some of us have," I told her because I couldn't tell anyone else.

"Sure," she said and started singing some old-fashioned song, with the line "I ain't got the blues." Then she stopped for a moment and said, "We just need to make some new memories."

I knew how the station worked. It was beautiful and familiar. I sat watching people, a woman in a large, brimmed hat clutched the arm of a younger man who pulled her along, a man with three dogs on a leash stopped to talk to anyone interested in the dogs, a grandmother in argyle socks and a windmill of a skirt sat waiting in a lawn chair, a mime juggled oranges near a newsstand. Did they see me as a tired old man capable of nothing? No trouble. Maybe that was why no one noticed me.

I knew what I wanted to do, which was the opposite of my dream the other night about leaving the boy on a train, so I did it. I followed a funnel of people and boarded a train myself. I hoped it was going somewhere I'd never been before. A city of subversively kind and attentive women, a city made of paper, one where no one owned a pen or pencil or anything to write with and everything blew away in the first wind. I would send myself away.

I knew how to avoid the ticket master, knew how the trains worked. There were so many rumbling and grinding noises, people settling into seats. I found one. I read all the ads above people's heads, about different kinds of help. I settled under the harsh light. When we started moving I saw the girl, Emily, at the station waving her arms frantically as though she'd just lost her favorite cat. She could see me fading away. I assumed someone from THEM would take care of Aaron if I never came back. I tried on that feeling. He would find some other home. I was one in a long line. They could have my apartment. I closed my heavily lidded eyes. I could pick up my retirement check any place. I could go to New Jersey, Michigan, Mexico. The city of sleeping children. No one would care. My hand gripped a bar and began shaking. Why should I be the one to run away? I needed to understand what happened with Martine and Phillip. I needed to discover why the boy affected me. I pulled the stop signal and got off at the next stop.

Aaron was with me. I couldn't get rid of him.

When I got back to the station, Emily was there in an orbital-patterned pants outfit with a space between the two pieces that exposed the rind of her stomach. She was resting her head in her hands, her notebook and pen waited patiently. I patted her on the head. "Hi Emily."

"I thought you were gone."

"No."

"I've thought about doing that too."

"Don't you have school?"

"My mother doesn't care if I go or not." Emily looked sad.

"Oh."

"I just don't know where to go." Her big, blue eyes focused on me. "What made you come back?"

I could hear other trains swelling toward us, then hurrying by. "I don't know. I guess I thought about everything I need to learn."

"If I got onto that train I wouldn't come back."

"Don't be so sure." But I didn't know her that well. I picked up her scribbled notebook. "Are you following me and taking notes?"

"Yes."

"Can I read them?"

"No." She confiscated her notebook and tucked it away.

"You really don't have anything better to do?" I reiterated. She shook her head and her thin, dark hair fell behind her large ears in clumps like dead grass. "Well, come up to my apartment. I might have a soda there somewhere. You can teach me what you've learned." We stood up, began walking.

I saw the woman, fat in layers of old clothes, her dirty arms spread wide, in a corner. A shopping cart missing one wheel crouched in front of her. Her rage lurched through her. She babbled about rain, rust, wars, and racism. I wondered if a whole city full of people like her existed, then how would anything get done? Her anger settled into harsh, filthy folds on her face. Emily and I walked past her. Her silhouette ranted and shook its fists. She bellowed insults that alarmed or embarrassed people at the train station. She was the woman from my dreams.

***

"I know some secrets," Emily whispered, turning toward me as she entered my apartment, flourishing her notebook.

I closed the extra bedroom door. "C'mon, everybody has secrets. What do you think mine are?" I went to the kitchen to make coffee.

Her shoes rested below the couch, abandoned pets. She consulted her notebook. She looked up empty. She frowned. "Maybe I was wrong. Maybe you ride horses naked under a full moon or lock up girls and make them recite French until they scream. Maybe you take apart small animals and make art out of them or make music from clock parts. It's hard to tell about people from watching their actions. I have to go by what my intuition tells me is inside of them."

"I'm just an old man. I don't have that much energy."

She wiggled her bare feet. "You don't have any pictures of people anywhere. It's so empty here, like you were just born or like you don't have a past, or maybe you're leaving soon."

"Here's a soda." I handed her the cold cylinder.

"I have to use your bathroom." She rose, barefoot.

"Wait a minute. I need to clean it a little." I rushed to the bathroom and threw the boy's tubes, bottles, pans, cotton balls, and the extra toothbrush, into a cabinet under the sink. I wiped a few surfaces. "Okay."

Just as she closed the bathroom door, the boy began making swallowing sounds. They grew louder and became moans. I hurried into Aaron's room and turned on the light. The boy was flailing. I gave him the pen and paper.

Vant to see girl.

"You know it's not allowed and you'll be removed from here if you don't behave." Would I have minded? The boy was all I had and I needed to learn how to care for someone again. I was finding it difficult. I could have threatened him with something worse. I understood that the boy was lonely. I wondered how much a person could hide. His body grew quiet, mushroomed out across the sheets. "I'll read more to you. I'll teach you how to write better. I promise." I couldn't interpret anything from his face. It reminded me of dead bees attached to his swollen body.

One blink. *Yes.*

I relaxed, left, closing the door. I could hear the garbled flush of the toilet, wings of water filling the sink, Emily turning the knob of the door. I turned the television on in the living room, which I'd been told not to do again because it imitated our lives in a distorted way and brought bad news from the outside.

My heart was beating fast as she graciously smiled, said, "Oh, I thought I heard something." She nodded at the television as if it was another person. She sat down again, put her twitching bare feet on the couch. "I like you, Jimmy. I don't know why. You're a strange old man."

"Don't you like any boys in your class?" When I turned off the television, people's faces grew to a pinpoint and then disappeared.

"I never want to become my mother."

"How about some girlfriends?"

"They've just learned how to hide their claws. I've still got scars to prove it."

A pause. "What do you like to do?"

"Sometimes I feel too big for my body," Emily said. We were talking about the mind. "My favorite thing to do when I'm alone is to try and remember everything I can about someone. I close my eyes. I try to remember hair color, clothes, the way they walk, talk, exactly what they said. Some of the kids at school think I'm weird 'cause I'll say, 'Hey, that's the opposite of what you said last week.' And they'll be all, 'How do you remember what I said last week?'" She smiled. "People hate having their inconsistencies pointed out to them. But what else do I have to do?"

"We all have our inconsistencies, even you, Emily." She made a pouting face, slipped her shoes on.

She was at the front door, ready to leave. "It's easier to see other people's. Point mine out if you ever see them," she said, probably not meaning it.

"I'll tell them hello." But she had already left.

***

I missed lunch that day with my friends at the diner where an older waitress spit watermelon seeds to the beat of whatever popular song she chose on the jukebox. I called Rosemary and said, "Let's bring Aaron to the meeting tonight." I would dress him up. I could make him into whatever I wanted.

"Why?" she asked, her voice trying to catch up with everything she was thinking.

"So he'll know what's going on. Why not? What else does he have to do? But I can't get him there alone. I want to dress him up and take him out. I need your help."

"I'll call THEM and see what they say."

"Do whatever you need to do."

She called me back. "After much discussion, the governing group said it was okay for tonight. I'll be over later to help."

I asked the boy, "What would you like to be tonight? A cowboy? A gangster? A Roman emperor? A skeleton?"

I thought of Phillip. I was a different man when I knew Martine. I remembered Halloween and dressing Phillip as a ghost, a black ghost, a boy in negative. Martine was excited. It was her first Halloween here. I waved at them as they walked down the street, a breeze blowing, leaves dashing from the trees, car lights and street lights pushing away all the darkness. Everything was escaping. I wanted to go with them, to see Phillip's small face as people said *yes* or *how scary*. I wanted to see the bags fatten as he accumulated candy and pennies and whatever else people were giving away. It was simpler then, with children in feathers, plastic, capes, carrying swords and guns and implements that lit up in the night, crisscrossing the streets and running up and down the stairs in apartment buildings. Now they hardly come at all, apples stuffed with razor blades, people who could snatch you, drugs and needles found strewn among the candy. I watched Martine, lit up with inviolable pride at the boy's costume and the promise of the evening, and it had filled me. Her hand moved down the slick white sheet, unable to hold on to any part of him. I imagined Phillip saying, *Hurry, let's go to the next place and the next one. More!*

Martine and I had kissed, deeply, while watching television, imitating lovers we had seen on the screen, bathed in a red sunset, margaritas in their hands, palm trees eclipsing them as they whispered endearing names to one another. It had felt sad, as though we were wishing for something we didn't have. I didn't feel like time was running out then, even though Martine had to do something about her husband. I waited for the two of them to return, experiencing my first episode of popcorn-sized pain floating through my head.

Aaron didn't answer for a long time. Maybe he was thinking about what he'd like to be. He could have been thinking about anything.

Finally he wrote. *Don want to go.*

That surprised me. I thought he'd be glad to get out. I was trying to be a better person with Aaron. "Why?"

Am Afraid what wil do to me.

"It's not Halloween. We don't have to dress you up. I just thought it would be fun."

Am Afraid.

"What are you afraid of?"

He closed his eyes, pretending to sleep.

***

Rosemary brought over a boy's black tee shirt and white pants. Of course. Her hair fell into gray commas around her face as she bathed and dressed the boy until he finally looked like everyone else from the group. "There. Absolutely perfect," she said about her own handiwork. The boy spent most of the time rolling his head back and forth, a perpetual "no." He had at first tried to push Rosemary away with his hands, but she had grabbed them with her own hands, splashed with age spots, as though dampened by rain. She didn't say a word. The boy stopped fighting her. "Good boy, Aaron," she told him.

Rosemary telephoned two men to come and help us lift the boy down the stairs and gently place him in the back seat of a black car. I could do it but I appreciated the help. I watched billboards, signs, and lights go by bit by bit. The city was wearing a new outfit, one that could only be seen at night. I noticed someone moving a mop in the middle floor of a tall building through a lit window. I saw a young woman blow a kiss to a man in a fedora hat beneath a street lamp, her heels clicking away. I thought about describing these scenes to the boy, but I knew he was supposed to be insulated from the outside world. The car radio had a lot to say until one of the men turned it off. The boy sniffed the air as if he could tell what was going on outside by smelling it through the crack in the car window. I closed my eyes, imitating the boy, and could hear rushing automobiles, people, buses, trucks, and the hollow sound of the streets. Our breathing echoed inside the black car. A dog barked somewhere, and then the car left it behind.

The meeting hall was full. I wanted to say, "Ladies and Gentleman, step up and consider what you have created," pointing to Aaron, who sat quietly in an adult chair. The man from the subway, with long, dark hair cascading around his shoulders, came to the podium. Everyone in the front wore the same thing to the meetings. Hair highlighted their differences. My mind made distinctions, fat, thin, blonde, brunette, old, young, skin color; unusual features, like a broken nose, stood out. A few of us in the back wore our street clothes, new people or the ornery, disgruntled, or stubborn. The man with long hair said that tonight was a special meeting about Aaron. Some people stood up and cheered. Aaron didn't express any emotions. He didn't move an inch and his face gave nothing away. There weren't the usual prayers, well wishes, readings, stories, interpretations, or lectures. There were testimonials from the sea of black and white, people popping up like performers from a circus:

"Aaron will shatter the small vase of our lives."

"He will be the voice of stones among us."

"He's the risk that's worth taking and he's the consequences."

"He's the space between our thoughts."

I pondered that last one. But still there were no clues to what they believed might happen. When I asked Rosemary later she patted my stiff, sore arm and said, "Aaron might only be a catalyst or he might be the event itself."

The man at the podium read, "At first everything was left to itself, to grow unfettered, to play or run wild. Animals and people understood one another and cooperated... That was a long time ago," he interrupted himself. He put his big voice back on. "Then a man came to show the world what more it could be. There were so many versions that people had to decide for themselves which way they wanted to go." The man looked up at all of us, his audience. "His name was Brian." The man held his arm out and a middle-aged, bald man in a suit that was too large for him took the stage. He wore thick glasses. He had a house-shaped jaw. An easy, practiced smile balanced on his face. His meaty hands froze in the air like birds shot from the sky and then landed on the podium. His expression said he didn't know exactly where he was. I'd seen that same startled look on Aaron. I wondered for a moment if Brian was blind. Then I remembered his thick eyeglasses. I was growing older and more forgetful by the minute.

I had wanted to meet Brian and there he was, but he wasn't anything like the powerful, omniscient man I thought he would be. He said, "I can't continue the story that we all know so well. It's all up to this boy, Aaron, who, like his Biblical namesake, is a speaker between the bureaucracy, or higher powers, and his own people. We will need him when the time comes, and he will tell us what to do. We are his humble servants." Brian bowed quickly. Then he stood up, spread out his arms and said, "Thank you all for coming." He stepped off of the stage to clapping and congratulations. I needed to know more.

I rushed toward Brian but two large, muscular men lifted me away. I was as light and empty as a bag of air. They noticed my street clothes. "I just want to ask him a question," I begged. They were ushering me toward the door. People stood at their seats and yelled encouragements at Brian. The men released me before we exited. I saw the entourage's backs and then I exclaimed, "I'm the one who takes care of Aaron."

Brian stopped in front of the door and turned. He held out his hand and shook mine. "I have to leave now but I think I have time for one quick question from such a good man. What did you want to know?"

There was so much. I had to think fast. "Is he related to you?"

"Yes," Brian answered generously. "I have many sons. All of God's children are related to all of us." He and his group departed grandly.

Aaron was in the same place I had left him, wearing his usual expression. So little of his life had passed so far. We were all tiny specks full of hunger running every which way. We were bound to run into one another sometime.

Chapter Five, Carly

I was in some fucking forest. My shopping cart was behind some fucking bushes and it was calling my name, my real name like it was lost.

Carly, Carly, a voice issued forth from somewhere in the middle of all my valuables.

"Shut up," I screamed.

Kathy, Lisa, Mary, it tried.

But I still didn't answer. What were we doing here? We were in the subway and then... No Things, no roads, nothing but vegetation. I was in someone's fucking dream. I pulled at my greasy hair, threw my old cap on the ground and stomped on it. Nothing helped. At least I could still say anything I wanted. The sky was looking down on me but it couldn't target me through the stoic trees. I hated all that blue. I sat on a pile of conventional green. There was a conference between me and the leaves. Branches. Flowers. Dirt. I missed the noise and rush of subway air that kept the voices somewhere else, the cement between me and filth. I didn't want to see the sun and its smeary self lighting up the back of everybody's head.

Where were all my friends and enemies? Where were the colored lights and masks the Things held in front of their real faces? I needed directions for once. I was distracted by the smell of coffee in the wind, the sound of grass, a maze of pale buildings I suddenly noticed in the distance. Did the town have entrances? I made a trail of twigs to find my way back to my cart and then I went looking for significant signs.

I thought I saw another Dis. It was that boy in his machine, in a clearing. And that girl, the Thing with awful blue eyes, was sitting near him in the grass. I was hiding behind a special tree while I counted my words, watching them. I took my gloves on and off. I could show myself what to see. Soon there would be stars. That lucky old man could help me if he was here. The boy was writing and the girl was reading.

Out loud she asked, "Where could we go? What could we be like?"

Quietly to the boy she said, "We haven't been gone long and every road looks like every other road. Maybe we should go back although no one will miss me." The boy blinked twice. "Well then," she continued, "you'd better tell me all of your secrets now."

"I know what you're doing," I screamed, unable to contain myself.

They looked at the tree, startled. I came out from behind my new friend with branches. I wanted to sweep them away with my impatient hands, but I knew them.

"We've been waiting for you," the Thing told me directly, and I had to hide my face in my hands to protect myself from her. I was afraid she'd already seen through me like the x-ray machine she was.

"Where's Jimmy?" I questioned them through my fingers, being good with other people's names.

"He's coming too," she said. But I had to dig deeper into

my special clothes to shield myself from her. Talking was hurting me.

The boy wrote something.

"I want to know whose dream this is," I tried. Silence. Then, "I need to go back," I let fly in their direction.

The girl, that Thing, shook her head.

"I've run out of ideas," I told them both. A three-legged dog hopped by and went deeper into the woods.

The Thing handed me the boy's notebook. *You can have some of my ideas, which include fire and water. Elemental ideas. West Woods is where everyone ends up sooner or later. It might as well be sooner.*

"You're hurting me." I missed my cart, my subway corner.

"We hurt people by mistake," the girl said just as the old white-haired man came crawling out of some bushes on his hands and knees. "We don't mean to."

The boy laughed but it was a grinding sound that frightened the old man holding flowers in his fists as he stood up.

"Look what I found growing in the part of the forest where the trees are thin and the limbs spread out way above our heads. There's so much moss out there. I was looking at the tree roots very closely. Sometimes they move." Jimmy tried to give us red flowers.

I wouldn't take any. I wouldn't touch them.

"You like it here, don't you?" the girl asked him.

"Yes, I've never been here before. It's so green and fresh. It feels like a new beginning," Jimmy answered.

"It does, doesn't it?" The Thing was clever and couldn't be trusted.

"I know what you're doing." I wasn't screaming.

"No, you don't," the girl snorted. "We don't know what we're doing yet."

The three-legged dog ran by again, stopped at the old man, smelled his pant leg. The dog peed on it, then ran toward the pale buildings.

"God damn it." The white-haired man tried to wipe his leg with leaves.

"We're not off to a very good start." Her blue eyes bored into the soil, reminding me of my soul.

"This fucking forest is inside my body." I could feel the start of shoots and seeds and saplings. Water, sunlight, and dirt were messing around. Trees, bushes, and grass leafed through my veins.

A man with no hair strode up to the clearing as if he knew his way around. Sunlight bounced off his naked head. He wore glasses. He kissed the boy on his puffy cheek. He patted the old man on the back, nodded at the girl. He glared at me, but I wasn't afraid of him. I moved closer to the group, threw my scarf on the ground.

"Brian," the old man called him, but it sounded like cursing.

"It's hard taking care of the disabled," the Thing explained, pushing the boy's machine around in little circles.

"Yes," Brian said, "but you are all so blessed."

"Where are we?" I screamed at him.

Brian stuck out his arm and violently pushed aside a shrub. There was an old, rotting, wooden sign that said *Welcome to West Woods, N.J.*

"If I can be here I can be anywhere," I yelled as loudly as I could, letting my spit fly and land on Brian's jaw.

CHAPTER SIX, JIMMY

"Adults don't have any imagination left," Don said, speaking about a new, oddly animated movie. "But kids get it."

My alarm had shrieked that morning, interrupting my dream, and I had just enough time to clean and feed the boy and meet Don, Jack, and Bill at the diner. What was a dream but a spy wanting to see what you already saw and making something out of it? It was creating something out of nothing that disappeared the moment you woke up. It was cotton candy.

"I wonder what goes on inside of a boy's head." One particular boy's head, which I didn't mention.

"You were a boy once," Jack said, handing the glossy, word-stained menu to the waitress, who winked at us.

"I liked books, even back then."

"You were weird," Don thumped his fork restlessly against his clotted napkin.

"Were?" Jack smiled. "Oh no, don't look, but that waitress, Susan, has a cut watermelon and she's heading this way." He dramatically threw his arms over his head to avoid being pelted by a spray of seeds.

"Have I told you the truth about Johnny Appleseed?" I inquired.

"Probably," Bill said, "but I get the feeling you're going to explain it to us again."

"How Johnny Chapman, which was his real name, got

the apple seeds free from cider mills and plant nurseries. It was 1806 or so and he was a missionary follower of the Swedenborg Church, which believed that the more you suffered in this world, the more you would receive in the next. Johnny Appleseed was happy as a wanderer who gave everything away and loved animals. He spread apple trees into Indiana, Illinois, and Ohio."

The waitress, Susan, put a disco song on the jukebox. Her cheeks were plump with watermelon seeds as she approached our table, her rhythmic hips swaying to the beat. I wasn't looking forward to the little righteous noise the seeds made as they hit our table and then had to be cleaned up.

"All I'm saying is that we all need to find something we like to do as much as Johnny did."

Jack said, "Maybe it'll find us."

***

Near the top of the stairs, close to my apartment, a thin, long-haired man and a blonde woman were wobbling around the inside of the building. Her too-blonde hair pointed in every direction and the man held her upright while he seemed to be tickling her in places I couldn't see. The woman wore a tight, white, too-short dress and high heels that made her lean on the man. They were laughing, slowly making their way down the stairs.

"What choo looking at?" The blurry woman slurred at me.

The man held her and nudged her forward by holding the back of her neck as though he was steering her. He pointed her smeared face at me, "Isn't she beautiful? She's the most beautiful thing I've ever seen."

Before I could reluctantly answer him the woman said, "Hey, old man, you can have my other arm." The woman pushed herself away from the man like a boat propelled out into the water. She offered me her available arm. "Don't be afraid. I'm not going to bite you." She laughed like she wanted to prove something. But she started to fall and the man caught her at her hip. I noticed her bad teeth. Wrinkles were edging her distracted face.

"Do they let you live here for free cause of your age?" she asked, her arms whirling around them both.

I didn't bother to answer her. I didn't know who she was pretending to be. "Aren't you Emily's mother?"

She and the man seemed to be whirring around each other in a sad sort of motion. "Yeah, maybe. So what? Is she bothering you?"

"No, she seems like a nice girl, just a little bit nosey."

"Tell me about it." She draped one thin arm over the man's shoulders. They were tipping to one side. "Just tell the girl to scram if she's bothering you."

"You look like her."

Emily's mother opened her mouth but nothing came out. She started to gurgle and then gag.

"Uh oh," the man said, quickly dragging her up the stairs.

She looked back at me once as if to say something, but

her hand flew to her mouth and, she hurried up the stairs with the man. They slammed the apartment door behind them.

***

"Martine, the woman I loved, had a son called Phillip. I bought him a small, yellow bird so he would have something that was all his and lively to play with. I thought it would be easier than a dog since I didn't have any pets growing up in the city. I was an only child and both of my parents were working so they didn't have time to take care of animals and they hardly saw me. I read a lot. I was certainly an unremarkable child." I smiled. The boy was there and not there, straddling the past and the present, the conscious and the unconscious. He was more and less than a boy.

I sighed, continued, "Phillip loved that bird and named it *Me*. What kind of a name is that?" I asked Aaron.

"'His English not so good as mine,' Martine said laughing.

"It was fine. It was his bird. Our conversations were, 'Did you clean Me? Did you feed Me? Are you going to let Me out of his cage?'"

Aaron, smiled, lying on his back in his bed.

"Martine got Phillip in school, and she was looking for a job. But sometimes I'd wake up in the middle of the night and find her gone. Sleepwalking. I'd find her downstairs at the door to the building. She looked like she was waiting, peering out the door, except that she was in her nightgown and she wasn't wearing any shoes. Once or twice I found her down the street near the fruit stand or on a stoop, her feet all dirty. I worried about her nocturnal wanderings.

"But Martine brushed it all off saying, 'Feet at home in dirt. It feel good.'

"'You might get hurt,' I said.

"'I like time together, all three, you, me, Phillip. We enjoy while can.' She smiled her usual smile. 'It no matter, this sleeping, walking. It go away.'

"She was right. She got a job and stopped disappearing in the evening. She was a night cashier at a fast food/gas store. Phillip used to let the bird out of its cage to fly around the kitchen while Martine was working and he was doing homework. 'Momma under de bad light,' was what he used to say about the place she worked. He stroked the bird beneath its beak, on its yellow feathers.

"One warm night I opened the kitchen window, not knowing the bird was resting on Phillip's shoulders and it flew out the window. I tried to catch it but it was a yellow breeze through my fingers. Me was gone, had taken off quickly into the hot city night. Phillip was heartbroken, wracked with tears, even though I promised him another bird.

"'No, Me everything,' he wailed. 'Where Me go?'

"I told him that the bird went to a very special place where no one else could go, no matter how hard they tried. I told him I'd get him another bird but Phillip wailed, 'No, Me, only Me.' I told him I'd take him to the planetarium.

"We went that week, just the two of us, his diminutive hand in mine, to the elevated dome in the park and watched constellations forming and reforming on the walls, supernovas splashed onto the ceiling. His head swiveled to see everything. We were engulfed by planets.

"'It makes anything seem possible, doesn't it, Phillip?' I asked.

"'Me come back soon,' he murmured his wish to the stars.

"I bought him another bird, which he never liked as much or trusted or named. After a few weeks it, too, disappeared one day. It took Martine and me a day to notice that it was gone. When we asked Phillip about it, he said, 'Maybe it go out, bring Me back.' He didn't want anything else but that bird."

I handed Aaron his pen and pencil. But he put them aside.

I scanned the newspaper, read Aaron an article about terrorists and their religion. I found a tiny article about Brian in the back, how he had evaded his taxes again this year and was being sued by the government. He might have to sell his boat. I wanted to show the boy how fragile all our worlds really were.

***

Rosemary came over early the next day and found blood that looked like dried rose petals on the boy's pillow. Both of his ears were bleeding. She cleaned everything up, sat in the living room, undoing and then rebraiding her long, gray hair. She was watching me drink coffee. "Did you do something we told you not to do?"

I slowly shook my head.

"We can ask the boy. I don't think he's capable of lying."

My mouth twisted. "I read him some of the newspaper." My stomach tightened.

"I'd ask you which part of it but it doesn't really matter. You know better." She wasn't angry. She chided me as if I was a child, patiently and tiredly. She had deep circles under her eyes as though her body was trying to bruise itself. "I have to call the doctor." She began searching through her large bag for the phone number. She dialed with great effort. "You know I could have had any job I wanted. And I chose helping Aaron."

"Why did you choose this?"

"He's a vessel and you have to be careful what you place within him." She looked at the floor. "You don't know what will emerge."

I closed the door to his bedroom but I wondered if he could hear us anyway.

"Don't underestimate him."

"We're all vessels, to an extent, and it depends on what we do with what we're given." I smiled, calculating the edges of her body under her flowing dress. What was holding her together? "Some of us are emptier than others."

"Aaron's different."

I wondered if they were actually afraid of him in some way. I briefly imagined the boy's bones loosening themselves, rearranging themselves inside his body. What would he become? The boy flying and falling and then trying again. They would take him apart, put him back together again. "We're all made of stories and it's a matter of how we interpret those stories."

"I can't disagree with you," she said.

There was a soft knock at the door and Rosemary answered it. The same doctor appeared. They murmured together, their heads tilted. I thought I heard the word "autism." He pushed his round glasses further back onto his nose. His shorn white hair had grown slightly since the last time I saw him. He was wearing the same white shirt and dark suit and carried the same cloth bag. Rosemary showed him into the boy's room and the doctor shut the door. He didn't say a word to me, as though I wasn't even there.

"Do you still want to take care of the boy?" Rosemary asked. Her braids were small, undone gray rivers of hair down to her waist.

"I don't really know," I answered honestly. I thought of his body as something that could crack and spill, his mind as some kind of structure that could either hold, toss, or break anything that entered it. My back ached at the bottom of my spine and, as usual, I tried to ignore it. Yet the pain kept on reminding me that it was there like someone suddenly grabbing me from behind. I wanted to twist the pain off, throw it away from me.

"How's your stomach, your rash, your head?"

"Better. Anything can be fixed," I declared. "In a fashion," I amended, thinking of the boy.

"Are you talking about your past?"

"No, that's done. All I can do is interpret that."

Rosemary laughed. "You sure are doing a lot of interpreting."

"I would have liked to save Martine and Phillip."

"I know," she said. "There are different ways to help someone. You've been coming to our meetings for quite a while now. Did you want to officially join us?"

"Not yet." Maybe it was me who was unsettled, unable to commit. My words ran alongside me, then ahead of me.

Rosemary made a huffing sound. Her face reminded me of broken ice.

But I was growing fonder of the idea of the boy, if not the boy himself. He was teaching me that I could take care of someone else, that, perhaps, I could be a better person.

"Once I took Phillip to the zoo, where we tried to watch the eyes of the animals. Phillip whispered *run away, run away* to the cats and bears. We watched for a reaction to our being there. We counted hyenas, smelled the stink of the flamingos' water, watched while the hawks and foxes were fed. We waited a long time for the snakes or lizards to move. I sat him at a bench near the kangaroos, told him he couldn't have any cotton candy yet. I went to the bathroom.

"When I came out he wasn't there, on the bench. When I yelled his name, it was hardly a word. There wasn't an answer. There was screeching near the monkeys. I ran over there. I wandered, calling him down winding paths until I finally saw him. Phillip was eating a cloud of pink cotton candy. A man hovered over him. The man was in his thirties, wore a trench coat, had a mustache, was smiling at the boy and half of his teeth were missing. He was about to place a hand on the boy's shoulder. I ran over, hugged Phillip.

"'Who's this?' the man asked Phillip.

"I thought I could see something glimmering in the man's pocket. 'He's my son. C'mon, Phillip, let's go.' I started to pull the boy away.

"'Phillip. So that's the boy's name,' and the terrible man began to smile. 'Whoa Phillip, are you sure this man's your father? You're different colors and he's pretty old to be your daddy.' The man positioned his hand on Phillip's shoulder authoritatively. He sounded like he didn't believe me.

"Phillip nodded, eating his cotton candy, unaware.

"'Didn't you hear me, son?' I asked. But I could hear how loud the monkeys were. The man's hand slipped off.

"'Hey, wait a minute, old guy. How do I know you're his daddy? You don't look anything like him.' He reached out for the boy again.

"I hit his hand away. 'Leave the boy alone or...'

"'Or what? I didn't do nothing but try and help a poor lost boy.' The frightening man laughed. 'There are boys like this everywhere. Boys that nobody wants. Boys left on benches.'

"'Fuck off.' I took Phillip's hand and started walking away with him as fast as my legs could move. I never knew I'd have to fight over him.

"'You fucking, stupid old man. You don't know nothing. You'll see, one day you won't be looking and pouf, the boy'll be gone. And you'll forget about him.' He mumbled, 'He'll be mine.' To the boy he said, 'Good cotton candy, huh? If you ever want any more, you know where to find me, Phillip.'

"My heart was racing. I was so relieved to get home with Phillip. I never told Martine how careless I had been with Phillip or how easy it was to lose him. She already knew those things."

Rosemary nodded as though she'd heard all this before.

The doctor emerged from Aaron's room. He closed the door behind him. Both Rosemary and I stood. He stopped me but didn't seem to remember my name. He gave me the usual instructions along with bandages, ointments, pills. He gave me a lecture on not sullying the boy again.

"Next time I'm called, I'll have to tell Brian directly. He won't be a happy man," the doctor told me ominously. He waved courteously at Rosemary and as he left, Emily slipped through the open front door.

"It sounds like there's a party in here." Emily was wearing speculative orange high heels, stockings with holes in them, and a very short skirt. "My mother brought home some real loser and he hasn't left the apartment since last week."

Rosemary looked horrified. "You have to go now, young lady."

"Who are you?" Emily sat on the couch, getting comfortable.

"That's none of your business. You have to leave this very minute." Rosemary looked at me as she pointed her finger at the front door.

Emily looked at me. I said, "You have to go, Emily. We're busy."

"But Jimmy, you don't look that busy," she whined, "and I hate it where I live. Can't I just hang out here for a little while?" She fiddled with her heels.

"No," Rosemary answered, "we're busy, and we need you to leave right now."

Emily stood up, her hands adjusting the air, "Okay, okay. I get it." She peered at me sadly. "One day," she said, wagging a finger, "I'll know everything." She left.

Rosemary stood with her fists on her hips. "That can't be allowed. News about the boy could go anywhere."

"Do you really think people would care?" I asked.

"Yes." Rosemary gathered her things hastily, pulled her hair back, heaved her bag onto her shoulder. "You already know what you should and shouldn't do." She went into the boy's room, left the door open. She bent down and kissed the boy on his pale forehead before she left.

I went to Aaron's room to close the door and I saw that he was crying, fat streaks that reminded me of wet glass, complicated and vulnerable. I wondered how long he had been crying. I had never had so many people in my apartment all at one time, except for the police, the time right after Martine and Phillip. I closed his door behind me as softly as I could.

***

That night I could only remember fragments of my dreams, something like an animal clawing its way out of my head, a knot at my back with nerves tangling into a ball that formed another person, a homeless woman who kept calling my name. The woman seemed to have something she wanted to tell me. Her name was Carolyn or Karen.

A cup of coffee moved me into a yellowish day with light brimming at the windowsill, raw pigeons that ate out of your hand if you offered them bread, cars cruising through city streets. I felt bristle on my chin. I thought of the pigeons that carried messages back and forth long ago, before we had so many other ways to communicate. They flew with notes attached to their feet. I began shaving in front of the mirror. When had I become so old? I wasn't sure I wanted to know.

Rosemary was blood in my mouth, a small cut I tried to find or leave alone. I couldn't do either one. The boy was quiet and seemed fine after yesterday. Moving him made my bones feel as though they were dissolving, which they probably were. I had both of us to take care of, do what was necessary. I watched clouds at the window, latching together, then drifting apart. I told the sky it was full of memories that no one cared about. I listened. I believed I could hear heartbeats nearby, through floors and doors, and all the city noises, cars, sirens, televisions, phones ringing, doors. I pretended to be the boy, listening intently to everything.

I tiptoed to my front door and threw it open. Emily was there, sitting on the steps, filing her pink fingernails. I wondered what a whole city full of teenage girls would be like, lots of giggling and boys.

"You can walk with me," I told her, "I'm on my way to meet some friends for lunch."

"What were you and that woman busy doing?" Emily smiled, a flexible, evil smile.

"You know, Emily, there are people you don't get anything from and ones who you hope will give you everything someday."

"Oh, that's what I thought." She looked down at the passing sidewalk.

"Do you have any boyfriends, Emily?"

"Well," she said, "there is this one boy at school, Hammer. He puts his arm around my waist sometimes between classes and he's so gentle. Sometimes I can feel his blood rushing around under his skin. It's just that he wants more, like you said. And I don't know." She shook her head, her blue eyes flashing under her black hair, her thin nose and big ears glowing. She was so awkwardly put together. I wondered if she would look like her mother someday.

"I met your mother."

"You poor thing. Did she say anything about me?"

"No, not really." We were nearing the diner.

"I hope she wasn't mean. God, I hope she didn't throw up on you. She's done that before." She stared at me.

"Well, Emily, we're here." We were outside the bullet-shaped building, all glass and steel. "Would you like to come in and eat with a bunch of silly old guys?" I waved at the guys at our usual table, which was bathed in a surge of weary morning light and scattered with haphazard glasses of water and silverware as I opened the door.

"Sure." And Emily was next to me, myopically heading toward the table.

The waitress was wearing white flowers in her blonde hair as she rotated around the counter. "Well, hi there, Honey," she said to Emily. "What a cute girl and so brave to join this group of old farts."

Emily smiled at her, squinted, and sat down near the end of the table.

"This is Emily, a neighbor of mine."

"Tell us a little about yourself," Jack said to the girl.

"I just met this boy called Hammer and I'm not sure what to do with him."

"You like him I take it?" Don was chewing already.

"More or less." She smiled easily. "Mostly more. School's the other problem because it's becoming so obsolete in my life." She was waving her arms, glad to have an audience.

"Here, Honey," our waitress said, placing a Coca Cola on the table, "on the house." She left to watch a noisy television in the corner of the restaurant.

Bill laughed. "It was obsolete in my life too and look what I became. I'm in the exciting field of stationary, desperately trying to make a living. So stay in school, Emily."

Emily started voraciously chattering about a girl's nose ring at school that she threw to a friend behind the teacher's back when our waitress gasped loudly and turned up the volume on the television.

"Henry Aimsworth, head prosecuting attorney for New York state, was killed an hour ago. He was the son of Brian Aimsworth, the notorious leader of THEM and a well-known tax evader. Henry Aimsworth had just given a speech at a charity luncheon for domestic violence victims when someone ran up to him on the street and shot him dead. The perpetrator was wearing dark clothes and a white jacket and yelled something unintelligible and then disappeared. Henry had left his father's group recently because of a rumored disagreement. There are currently no leads as to the identity of the shooter. The shooter's motive is also unknown and so far no one has taken responsibility for the killing." The newscaster showed an old, grainy photograph of Henry with his arm around Brian. "If you know or have witnessed anything please call the police or this station immediately."

Chapter Seven, Carly

I was listening to my body, filled with food, laughing. It was hilarious. Good hot food, not stuff from garbage cans. I rubbed the room walls, trying to erase the odor. It was warm but stuffed with the smell of Things and more Things and no train breeze to take it away. I followed the lucky old guy, Jimmy, here, to this restaurant. They fed me in some room out back as long as I left my shopping cart and valuables outside. They fed stray cats lining the alley too. Pointy bones, shiny fish scales and rotten vegetable tops, plus empty cartons, overflowed the garbage cans. I could hear two cats fighting over some scrap.

"I know what you're doing," I yelled once at the big guy that gave me a plate with lumps on it. Then I held my lips together with my gloves.

"Yeah," he laughed, his white apron streaked with something green. "I'm feeding some crazy lady."

"I'll get lost. Then I'll get lost," I circled myself in the tiny room, "inside my body."

"You do that," he said and turned around and went back into the steamy, noisy kitchen.

I ate as fast as I could. I could hear the Things inside, chewing their food like cows. It was good. It was very good. I saw a picture of Brian flash across their TV. I held onto my head, trying not to let his thoughts come through. The bad ones. But they went through my fingers. *Me, knocked down, onto my knees by a large Thing and Brian talking to my hair. They were angry and I could feel the vertical bruises. Something grabbed my hair, pulled. Me?* My knit cap was too nice to keep the words out. *"Here," and a bag of food was in my arms. A Thing telling me my thoughts were dangerous and I could hurt myself and others. I had the scars. Brian told me to leave him alone.*

I licked the plate, saw a mean, creased face with pokey hair and left the plate and person on it at their doorstep. I grabbed my cart and wandered. It was an area I wasn't used to. The garbage cans didn't have much to tell me, a little gossip about nervous birds. A curly man left something behind, and when I went to see what it was, the space around me was filled up with canaries. I tried to move my arms, but they only fluttered yellow. I couldn't tell if it was night or day. I knocked some onto the cement by accident. Their bones snapped. I stopped moving, spread my arms out. I turned around and around. The rest gathered along the lengths of my sleeves and hollow body, trying to nest inside me.

"I don't mean that much to you," I told the chirping birds, and they left. I wasn't their Brian.

The killing noises were getting louder and heavier all around me. I saw a friend. He had blood on his shirt and food hidden somewhere that sprayed out from his mouth. He was screaming at the buildings all around us. He went to his pile of blankets. He had three empty bottles next to the lump that looked like a person. I shuffled around the blankets.

"No cart," he motioned.

So I parked my shopping cart a few feet away, yet easy to get to. His eyes were worn stones and dead dog bones held him together. So he told me. It looked like water was moving his shirt around when he talked. He was excited, reaching for me.

"No touching. Ever," I yelled.

"Come look. See what I found." His words were not for everyone, only me. "It sounds like bees."

But I was afraid to see what was hidden in his blankets. "I know what you're doing."

"Sooner or later everything flies," he said more quietly. His pants were falling down, but his shirt covered up what I didn't want to see. Pieces of him scattered around like birds. He was digging through his blankets.

"I don't want a drink," I said.

"I'm not giving you one. Hold out your hand for a surprise."

I held out my gloved hand and closed my eyes. He placed something hard, heavy, and metal in my palm. My arm fell, because of the weight, and then rose again.

I opened my eyes. "I'd heard of this." I stared at it, wanting to run my tongue all over it. "It makes ghosts."

"Yeah," he said, "Those ghosts are pests. They never leave me alone. Now give it back." He held out his empty hand.

Chapter Eight, Jimmy

My television declared that Sarah Gerard, a housewife who had an important position at THEM, had been killed that morning on her doorstep while her two small children were leaving for school. No one knew who the shooter was. No one heard anything until the shots or saw anything.

"Is this the beginning of the end?" I asked Rosemary.

"Yes," she said. "It's been predicted. There will be changes."

I had woken up with a jolt that morning as though someone was moving their hands around in the lining of my stomach. But I had stopped having so many dreams. It was better to focus my energy on the real world. Luckily, Rosemary came early.

"I need to know more."

"No, you don't." That was all she said, ignoring me, readying the boy for his bath.

"Why can't there be good things like water into wine or money made from stones or people raised from the dead? You know, real miracles. Desirable stuff made out of nothing."

"Who says everything's bad? It's all how you look at things. You guys always need proof and can't commit."

"How can you commit to something you can't touch?" I touched her shoulder.

Rosemary actually smiled at me. "I haven't been touched in a long time."

I wrapped my arm around her back and kissed her. One long, gray braid ran down her back like fingers. It was soft in my hand. She didn't pull away. Her lips were warm and moist and tasted like minerals. I wasn't thinking about my healed hip, hurt knees, weak heart, dissolving wrists and ankles. I wanted to fly or plant myself and grow tall. She pulled away.

"I don't want any more than is necessary." She was pushing her palms against my chest. "Not right now anyway."

I couldn't help smiling. "That's fine with me. I'm a patient, old man."

"Please leave me alone with the child," she requested. "I have much to ask him."

***

"Go back where you belong," one from the group of white men yelled at Martine from across the clearing in the circular park. Trees stretched around us comfortably, green grass reached everywhere except the cement paths. We were walking down one of the sidewalks toward a grove. It was early morning and empty.

"Where's that?" I screamed in his direction, with enough distance between us. But the clot of men turned toward us.

"And you," another man pointed at me. "What are you doing with her? Can't you find one of your own kind?"

"Like one of your incredibly charming wives?" I grabbed Martine's hand and we ran, away from the men, past trees and trembling bushes. We hid behind a car in a nearby parking lot.

"Why?" Martine whispered to me behind a bumper. We couldn't see the men following us although we waited, crouching, for a while.

"Because they were big and strong and there were too many of them." I held her chin, kissed her cheek. "They only care about what they see on the outside of people."

"No, Jimmy. Why talk to them men at all?" She asked me wisely.

***

The subway station reminded me of night, lit by fluorescents, connected together by tunnels. Day sped through them, with bright and busy headlights, in a hurry to move along the tracks. I tried to concentrate on ads plastered onto the curving tunnel walls because, maybe, they were trying to tell me something. Something I was missing.

I had suppressed my urge to follow Rosemary from my apartment. I really didn't know much about her. Where she lived. What she did when she wasn't involved with THEM or her mother or us. But that kind of act had consequences. I had learned that.

Metal doors opened, thrusting people in and out. A little girl with blonde ringlets exited. When I looked over her head, I saw an ad for a moment before it rushed by. It said: **Come Fly with Us**—an ad for acrobatic training with a young girl whose legs and arms were twisted into an inconceivable position. I closed my eyes and imagined the boy held up by his arms, his useless feet dangling in the air. It would be more than he'd ever known. I wasn't sure it was possible. But, maybe it would set his life into motion like winding a clock, his heart roaring, his blood murmuring. It was analogous to love. He would be pushed out of himself. They were overprotective at THEM and he needed jostling.

What did Rosemary need?

I looked for THEM but I didn't see the usual people. A woman in a pink dress daintily led a small dog on its leash around the subway platform and then exited, scooping up poop elegantly. A man was carrying a baby strapped to the front of his dark suit. Two people were gesturing to one another excitedly, and then I realized that they were deaf. Their hands were lovely and expressive, their faces animated. A woman's back with Martine's beautiful loose black hair was about to step into a train. I tapped her on the back and when she turned around, she had a face older than mine.

"I'm sorry," I said, "I thought you were someone else." I knew it couldn't be Martine. But something was jagged inside of me.

"You made me miss my train."

"I'm sorry."

Then I saw the bag lady huddled under layers of comical clothes in the dim light under the stairs. Natasha. Her shopping cart was overflowing. As I moved closer I saw that she had plastic roses in her hair, not her usual knit cap. Sometimes I wondered whether I was asleep and dreaming of her or awake. Some days I couldn't tell the difference.

I sat on a bench near her, along the cement side of the stairs, facing away from her. "Have you ever cared about anyone?" I asked her shadow behind me.

"He passed through me," she whispered instead of her usual screaming.

"My desire makes me afraid," I confessed to her. "It hasn't led to anything good in the past, only heartbreak and sorrow."

"They splinter you. Then they drop the moon onto the ground and forget to pick it up." Her skittish voice darted all around in the dampness behind me.

"I keep on thinking about her mouth," I said.

"It's no good. It'll kill you."

"You're probably right." Why was I talking to a homeless woman? I didn't know but some of what she said made sense to me.

"I loved Martine and her son a while ago. I took a late lunch one day from the station and was walking to see Martine at her job. As I got closer to the enormous windows of the overlit convenience store where she worked the doors shuffled open, letting people in and out, I could see Martine behind the counter. She was talking excitedly to a man, and her hands were swirling in the air. A smile overtook her face, a smile I hadn't ever seen before. I could only see the man's back, but he was big and brawny and had short, dark hair. Then she leaned across the counter and kissed him. Their lips met. The man put his arms around her. She put her arms around him. I turned away.

"Later that night or maybe it was the next morning I

asked her, 'How was work?'

"'Good. It good,' she gave me a little smile. 'Phillip and I no know what we do without you. Thank you, Jimmy. You a good man.' She touched my cheek.

"But she didn't tell me anything about who the man was or what he was doing there. And it festered inside me. It got worse because she didn't say a word about it. I even tried to ask Phillip if he knew something about his mother meeting a man. He looked up at me hopefully and asked, 'Maybe it my father?'

"'Phillip, you know your real father is gone and he was from the islands. You were really small when he died.' I didn't mean to be so blunt.

"Phillip's face looked chewed. 'I no like other father here.'

"'The one you used to live with?' He nodded. I kissed the top of his tiny head that smelled like crayons.

"I didn't ask again but it bothered me. I wasn't sure I could trust her. Things deteriorated. I found myself following her when I could, when I wasn't taking care of Phillip. To the grocery or drugstore and I didn't catch her with him again. But maybe they were clever.

"Until one day, a few weeks later at breakfast, she mentioned that her husband had been by to see her at work and that they were tentatively friendly again. He found someone else and was going to divorce her, and that he was drawing up the papers right now.

"'When did he come by?' I asked.

"'A few week ago. It good news, Jimmy. Happy news.'

"I wanted to ask what he looked like but I couldn't. 'You should have told me earlier.'

"'I want to know that he do it. Not just words.'

"Relationships are such fragile, difficult things, Natasha. I don't know why I'd even be thinking about another one."

The woman in the shadows jumped toward her shopping cart. "I know what you're doing," she screamed.

"That's funny," I said, "because I don't."

***

When I returned home Rosemary was gone but she had left a note. It said: *You're a wonderful man, Jimmy, but there isn't going to be anything between us. Certainly not right now.*

"Aaron," I said, going into his bedroom, "did you and Rosemary have a chat?" I retrieved his paper and pencil from a dresser drawer as he blinked once. *Yes.*

"Did she tell you how much I like her?"

He blinked once.

"You were the last one to talk to her. Did you advise her not to see me, at least right now?"

Two blinks.

"What did you tell her?"

SEE wha will happen

"From now on I'm giving you lessons on English and writing. I also want to talk to you about something you might enjoy doing. It's called acrobatic training where you hold onto other people and fly through the air, at least when you're strong enough."

His filmy eyes widened. *Ask Them*

"I will. I want to ask someone else to come along too."

Rose mars

"No, not her. I'll be back in a minute."

It was a whim but I clasped my way up the stairs and knocked. The woman who opened the door was disheveled and drinking. She was barefoot and a plastic fork was stuck to the back of her hair, which zigzagged around her face. "Is Emily here?"

Her face changed as she came to recognize the name, slowly. "Yeah, Emily, come out here." She focused on me. "You're the downstairs neighbor." One finger and the fist around her bottle wagged at me. "I remember you." The bottle carved the air between us.

Emily emerged in a demure skirt down to her knees, socks, flat shoes, and a button-down blouse. She saw me. "Oh, hello, Jimmy."

"Did she do something?" her mother inquired.

"No, I just wanted to show her something she might be interested in."

"It better not be something dirty or disgusting." Her mother laughed deeply and started hiccupping. She sipped from her bottle.

Emily pushed her aside. "No, mom, he's normal." She twirled around in her clothes, a plaid skirt down to her shins, knee socks, a white blouse. "How do you like my clothes? I want to look like everybody else for a while until it gets boring. I borrowed these from a girl at school. She's very Catholic."

"I like them. You look lovely, Emily. I want to show you something."

"Okay, I'll be back soon, mom."

"Don't do anything I wouldn't do." She laughed again and shut the door, her bottle clinking against the wall.

We made our way down the stairs. "I wanted to show you my secret, Emily. But you have to promise not to ever tell anyone." We entered my apartment. My bones were creaky and sounded like the rusty hinges of my door.

"I don't have anybody to tell." She smiled. "I promise. I knew you had a secret. Out with it, Jimmy."

I sat her down on the sagging sofa in the living room. I began, pacing around the room. "I'm taking care of a boy and the noises that you've heard are from him."

"I haven't seen a boy." She stared at me with those sky blue eyes as though she already knew. "Is he your son?"

"No, I'm taking care of him for a while. He's mute and blind and he doesn't have use of his legs so sometimes you might hear his wheelchair or the strange noises he makes. His name is Aaron."

She was looking around the living room as if he might come barreling out of a room and she'd need someplace to hide.

"If you tell anyone I'd probably have to disappear."

"I promised and I mean it. You're still a bit mysterious. Whose boy is he?"

"He's in my spare bedroom. He communicates by blinking his eyes or by writing on a pad that I only give him when he needs to use it. One blink is for yes and two is for no. He can hear well. He can probably hear us right now. I think he's heard you before and wants to meet you." I sat down in a chair. I felt as if my choices weren't my own. How to explain Aaron? "It's a long story but I thought you might help me take him outside."

"Sure," she said nonchalantly. "Can I see him?"

I opened the door to his room. "This is Aaron." Emily followed me inside. She didn't seem surprised by the boy's appearance. He was in bed on his back, as usual. His filmy eyes were open and unseeing. Sheets and a bedspread reached toward his neck. His dark hair was newly shorn, glistening against his pillow.

"Aaron, this is Emily."

He moved his head precisely toward her and blinked once as though he already knew.

His pasty hands reached out so I brought him his pen and paper and he wrote: *jimmy go Now.*

"Aaron asked me to leave. Is that okay with you, Emily?"

"Sure, go ahead."

The boy wrote something down and handed it to her.

"Holler if you need anything." I was uncomfortable leaving her with the boy, but what could the boy do? I pulled up a chair for her. Her face twisted and then it softened. I left the door ajar, picking up his written notes, scattered all over the floor from this morning. They were left from his visit with Rosemary.

In the living room I looked at them. They said, *Lov and hate; we liv in brokin glass world; one stone begin; thing get worse, then better;* and *yes, for jimmy.* I wasn't sure what the questions were.

I fiddled around the kitchen and picked up a book. The girl was in Aaron's room for a long time. I had to knock because the caregivers would be coming soon. "Time to go." The boy was propped up in the bed, furiously writing. Emily sat primly with her borrowed skirt pulled over her knees. Her chin rested on her fist as though she was awaiting the boy's latest words. The boy deserved some kind of life, but I wasn't sure I was doing the right thing introducing them. I escorted Emily out of the room.

"Fascinating," she said at my front door. "He's like a puzzle."

"He can probably hear us."

"I forgot." Her hand flew to her mouth.

"People are coming." I opened the door.

"Can I come back and see Aaron?"

"Sure."

I opened the front door. She was clutching a pile of papers that the boy had scribbled on, including the last page he had cautiously held out to her. She was reading it when the boy began a terrible low moaning sound. "We'll try and have a little adventure with him sometime soon."

"Okay." But she was absorbed in the papers. "We were talking about the future. But I don't really understand everything he's trying to tell me. He wrote something about Rosemary and something about a fire."

"Can I see it?"

"Maybe next time. He told me that I need to try and figure it out. That's why I have to come back." She stuffed the papers into her purse.

I watched Emily's plaid skirt scurry up the stairs in time to hear her mother call, "Emily, Emily. I need help with these dishes."

"I'm on my way," her voice skipped upward.

I wondered who was the lion and who was the lamb.

***

When I walked into the diner, I noticed that although Don, Bill, and Jack sat together, eating, they positioned themselves as if each were alone. Old white men fidgeting with napkins, hunched into their clothes, lifting spoons and forks with gnarled hands. I could see their individual futures: one by ambulance, one tramping into the forest and never coming back, one crushed by a car he had been working on. I slid into my usual seat.

"Where's the girl?" Bill asked.

"In school I hope."

"Don was saying he wants to live in a town that isn't as big as this city."

"I had a dream last night that I was a fish," Jack said. "Do you think it's something religious?"

They were talking at one another all at the same time. The waitress came by, said, "That girl needs to learn to be a girl. 'Cause who wants to be a woman before her time? You need to tell her, Jimmy, that she has time to grow up." Then she winked at me.

"Hey, I like grown women," Jack made sure she heard.

"Just keep it that way," the waitress blew a kiss at all of

us.

"What do you think God looks like? Some old guy who looks just like Don, except with longer hair?" Jack asked.

"I dreamt I was a fishing boat once," Bill tried to help Jack.

"Why should I stay where I am? I could live someplace where you could practically grab the moon with the sky being so big, where I could get a house with a creek running through the backyard." Don started on his hamburger, ketchup oozing onto his plate.

"What would you do there?" I asked him.

"Nothing, same as I do here."

"So why move?" Jack inquired, sprinkling salt into his soup.

"I met a woman." I tossed it out there, onto the table.

"Ooh," the waitress said, flinging down several plates, "it's been a long time, Jimmy."

"Yes, it has been."

Don, Jack, and Bill were speechless for a while.

"Who is it?" Jack finally asked.

"Nobody you know. At least not yet. I'm still working on it."

"If I was a fish," Jack replied to Bill, "I sure wouldn't want to be on your boat."

"I could see the stars at night if I lived in the country," Don said.

"But there aren't good restaurants or movies out in the country," Bill said. He had known Don the longest.

"In my dream I was swimming through water, happily, until I bumped into the end of the lake." Jack frowned. "Then the sky was going to eat me."

"Maybe it's a sexual dream." I smiled. Jack didn't.

"It's probably about what we might do in a bad situation," Don said.

"Or lack of time." Jack was grumpy.

"That's why we need the girl," Bill said.

The waitress blinked her eyes, made her mouth into the O of a fish, and smacked her lips. Jack wouldn't look at her.

"It's not funny," he whispered. "There are nights when it's just the fish dream over and over."

"So when is Emily coming back?" Bill asked me.

"Yeah," Don said. "She's the one with a future."

"I don't know. Soon probably."

"We're lucky to still be alive," Jack said.

The waitress closed her eyes, moved her mouth like a fish again. Jack looked away from her.

"Except for Jimmy," Don said, "he might have something new coming his way."

"Maybe you should move somewhere, Don," I said, "someplace quieter, more restful."

A policeman came into the diner, ringing the bell on the door. He went to the counter, talked to the waitress. Sky froze in the mirror behind her and light fell onto the linoleum floor, resting where it landed. It was comfortable and didn't want to move.

"I'll tell you what, Jack," Bill said, "let your fish float near my boat tonight and I'll protect it and make sure nothing will harm it."

Jack groaned. "Why can't things be the way they used to be?"

It was a rhetorical question.

"Hey, you should invite your new woman friend to the diner."

Bill had made a hole in the middle of his pancakes and was eating them from the inside out.

"When it's the right time I will. And it might be a while."

"I hope not," Don said, cheerily stuffing a sandwich into his mouth, chewing.

They were my conscience, my advisers, my Greek chorus. They were familiar doors. I could walk through them at any time.

"I'll watch for your fish tonight and sing songs to it," Bill said to Jack. "I'll tell it where the end of the lake is. I'll tell it to watch for the moon on top of the water to guide it."

"Are these dreams all you think you have left?" Don asked.

"I hope not," Jack and I said at the same time.

***

I was alone with the boy and not alone. More and more people knew about him. He had been growing fat earlier because of how I cared for him. Now he seemed to grow complicated. He lied. He was capable of hurting others and himself. I needed to find out what else he could do. I could never be sure how much he really understood about people. Yet he made proclamations. His writing was improving rapidly. But I never knew what would come out of him.

Today he wrote: *I hear two boys on bicycles. They make bird sounds while talking about a girl. They say her chest is the size of two pebbles.* What had he overheard? I stared at his filmy eyes, long lashes, his pale body growing leaner. He was growing up isolated but he could hear everything.

Last week he wrote: *The man across this street took pills. He's a vegetable now.*

"What man? Where exactly?"

A man whose glasses fell onto the floor. Third floor, last apartment.

I ran over there, found the manager, and when we opened the man's apartment door it stank so much I left, going back quickly to my own apartment.

What is death?

"When we aren't here anymore."

That man's body fell down. It's still here.

"His body will disintegrate soon. Death is when we aren't alive or moving. Something has left us."

Am I dead?

"No." I could see his point though.

Something left me long ago. Will I die?

"Yes, eventually everyone dies."

I don't want to. What is it I need to keep inside?

"Some people call it a soul."

Where is it located in the body?

"Everywhere."

The boy tried to laugh soundlessly. *Then I don't think I had one to begin with.*

A few days ago he wrote: *I see pictures behind my closed eyes. One is a town with pink and blue houses. Another is Brian in a pool of blood.*

"Are you angry at Brian?"

No, but other people are.

He wrote: *I want to see Emily.*

"We don't always get what we want. And Emily is your only friend."

You have Rosemary.

"No, Aaron, I don't."

You had Martine.

"That's true." As if he needed to remind me. "But she's dead like the man across the street."

Who do I have?

Before I was going to lie he scribbled something quickly on his pad.

Get door. They here.

A knock at the door. Two women entered, neither was Rosemary. One woman was about twenty, with red hair and dark make-up around her eyes. The other was about forty, maybe the redhead's mother, and she wore a suit and high heels and seemed to be in a hurry.

"Oh, you're so old." The older woman seemed surprised.

"Is that a problem?"

"No, she didn't tell us. Rosemary called us last minute to come and take care of the boy." She looked around. "I had to leave work to get here. Where is he?"

I pointed to his room and the older woman went inside, her heels clicking a little path. The younger woman stayed outside, sat on the couch.

"They really only need one person. I'm the chaperone. Also I can help with the heavy lifting. My mother isn't too good with that, with or without heels." She was looking around my apartment. "You don't have much furniture here, do you?"

"What did Rosemary tell you?"

"Not much. Just to come."

"For how long?"

"I think just this one time."

I smiled. "Did she say why?"

"She said she wasn't feeling well."

"You two don't seem like the typical people I usually see here."

"Oh, and what is typical?" She smiled and her braces glimmered.

"The other people seem more devotional. Quieter." It was my turn to smile.

"You're right," she looked at a piece of paper, "Jimmy Hatfield. We're more like contractors."

Before I had a chance to ask her more questions, the girl's mother called her to help. The girl smiled with a frightening luminescence, raising her palms and shoulders into the air, and said, "You never know who's going to show up."

CHAPTER NINE, CARLY

I was inside the old man, Jimmy's, head and I needed to get out. There were cobwebs, dust, kisses, children, large, empty spaces, and blue gloves. Some Things turned their heads to face me, awful icons and revelations that made my skin wrinkle: the Dis writing in his notebook; the windshield of a truck cracked by a yellow bird; a boy and a woman running out of a building as fast as they could. *Wake up,* I wanted to scream. Maybe I did scream. *I don't want to eat your old man's brain.* Brian stole mine so that only a small patch of yard grass and a modest house from someone else's childhood remained.

I was bad to be around that day so I got out of his head and went to the park to sit on a bench, play Ring-Around-the-Rosie with pigeons. The afternoon didn't know what I wanted yet. Pigeons and I were hovering and pecking. There was a hole in the sky so the pigeons had the advantage. I grew angry. I was yelling at the place where some clouds met. Two boys came along on bicycles, singing some kind of stupid song. The trees tried to tell me something but I couldn't hear them. I pulled out my friend's small pistol instead.

I said, "You don't live here. I do." Maybe I was screaming. I shot a pigeon and it danced for a while among tree leaves and then fell to the ground and stayed. The tree grew quiet. The boys were upset and bicycled away. That made me happier.

Then I saw one of the dead men and he was running toward me, a policeman was with him. Pigeons cried and scattered, flying away. There was suddenly a smell, like smoke, from the gun after I pointed it at the dead men. But they kept on coming toward me. I tucked the ghost-maker into the clothes under my coat, and I ran, leaving my cart behind. I was sure pigeons would pounce on my cart but I had to run through the underbrush to the location where my friends waited out bad weather.

I tried to be quiet as I hurried, twigs and pollen fumbling on my ski cap. My clothes caught by the fingers on branches. I went up a slight hill and stopped on a rock, listening to the ground, trees, bushes, anything from the lake. I couldn't hear them following me. I waited to be sure I'd lost them. I peeled off my gloves and slipped them back on. I put my hands over my mouth. It was so hard not to say anything. I sat there for a long time with my fists stuffed into my mouth hole.

I waited for the stars, for the moon that came from the wrong direction. They had always been rude at night. But tonight they were more polite. I carefully made my way back to where I'd left my cart. I passed a tree with dark qualifications, flowers where there wasn't a grave, a red, plastic cup full of someone's beer dreams, a bush bent by a body. I could see the silhouettes of Things and dead people walking under the streetlamps. The moon tried to expose them, empty air, dark shapes cramped into small spaces.

My cart was gone. I wasn't surprised. It was now mulch for pigeons or eaten by gravity. I was missing my maps, two rows of fake teeth, extra clothes, a game board with palm trees, a doll with her arms reaching, extra clothes and pillows, a shattered photo of Brian.

I had to go to the secret place. It was near the freeway, under a bridge. I followed the sound of cars. There were certain motions I had to go through and lots of fake stones. I threw a sweater down where some tree roots couldn't go further into the park.

"The she is you," a man's voice said from behind a bush. His outline was lumpy.

"No," I said, knowing about this, "I can chop these down, lay them flat." I lifted my palms.

"There's no horizon here, you know." He came out, had a smashed head with some blood and soil.

"I know." I turned toward him with a face that had been left outside too long. I picked up rocks. I had the ghost-maker, which could flash and disintegrate him. I had my fists too.

"I moved to this neighborhood but it has boundaries," he said, standing still.

"I'm outside, in the free world."

"Maybe," he said, "this is the land of lost chances." He laughed weirdly.

"I know what you're doing," I couldn't help myself, "and it doesn't have any meaning."

"What have you got?"

"A dead man took my cart. Now I don't have anything."

"I bet you could afford me." He smiled showing his missing teeth. He took a step closer. I threw my rocks at him. He stopped. He didn't look any redder.

Another blurry figure that resembled a tree came near us, which would tip the scale. A man's voice emerged, "Let her be, Fred. Them's the rules here."

Fred looked disappointed. "He's you and you're a crowd." Fred left.

"There's a lot of whimpering here," I said. "Do I need an umbrella?"

The newer man looked at me. "You don't need nothing to stay here. I watch out for things. You'll be okay here. Yell if you need me." He smiled with black teeth, which was a good omen. "But not too loud."

I lay down on the tree roots, spreading out my coat. I didn't want to be absorbed.

"This here's the place when there's nowhere else to go." The man nodded at the ground, turned around and left.

I thought about the sky and how it could hurt me. I was shriveled. I would have to go back to the subway, with its action noises and all those high, low, hidden, open spaces. The Things weren't as dangerous there. The policeman wanted a second chance but I wouldn't let him see me bleeding.

Just before I fell asleep, one of the men was near my ear and whispered, "You is a crowd. Tree roots go everywhere."

"Don't pull them," I told him loudly.

Then quiet was happening.

Chapter Ten, Jimmy

I wanted to argue with someone about Rosemary. Truth be told, I liked arguing. Or I wanted to, minimally, get her phone number, address, or some information about her. I didn't want to let her shut me out of her life. I wanted to see what would happen between us. First there was the boy. I performed a quick sponge bath, bathroom duties, combed his hair, brushed his teeth.

I tried calling someone. "I want to talk to Rosemary. I don't know her last name, but she helps me with the boy, Aaron."

"Who?" the woman's voice on the other end said, "I don't know which Rosemary you're talking about."

"The one with gray braids. She usually wears soft, plaid clothes."

"Oh." The woman's voice stopped for a moment. "But I can't just give out people's information to anyone."

"You can call me back. Look at your list of people being helped. My name is Jimmy Hatfield. You know me. I've been to many of the meetings. I'm the elderly man with Aaron. The ornery one."

"I'll have to check with someone."

"You do that." And I hung up the phone.

I waited for a while. I made too much coffee. I folded fragrant clothes from the laundry, watched jittery birds looking cramped on electrical wires that crisscrossed the streets. From my window I followed the tops of people's hats as they roamed the neighborhood. A brown scarf blew across the sidewalk, finally curling around a streetlight. Wind couldn't help me but it could get into people's apartments and throw things around without getting arrested. But I needed information. I checked on the boy, whose surface rose and fell evenly. I couldn't tell if he was asleep.

Aaron lifted his hands. I gave him pen and paper. *What does Rosemary have to do with anything?*

His English was better. "Are any of us important?" In winter we were all stuck inside, brooding, cold, imagining better health, and watching the afternoon lumber around, waiting.

Another woman called back. "What do you want Rosemary's phone number for?"

"She left something here while she was taking care of the boy. I also need her address." It was a comfortable lie.

"Well I hope that I'm doing the right thing. This is a bit of a leap." Then she gave me the information.

Was Rosemary a concept? Did Martine represent love? Was Rosemary who I imagined her to be? She wasn't any easier than me. My stomach clenched in a blasphemous way and a few tufts of my white hair fell onto the dusty edge of a window sill in my excitement.

I told the boy, "I'm going to call Emily. Let's have a little adventure." I could have left him there alone. What kind of trouble would Aaron get into? But I didn't know how long I'd be gone.

I remembered showing Martine and Phillip through a natural history museum. Phillip was bored. It wasn't Martine's history but she was polite and patient as we passed by dioramas with stubborn versions of the American past. Phillip liked to touch objects and there was finally a sea exhibit with starfish and crustaceans that he could position and give names like Curly or George.

Martine and I were holding hands. "I go away. Take care things," she explained. Phillip was studying a mummy, encased first in bandages, then stone, then in glass. He followed us.

"What things?" We hesitated at the fragile butterflies, then dinosaur bones the height of ribbed houses. We peeked in an exhibit about the brain. We kept on walking.

"Money things. Things Jimmy no need in him life," she stated. People walked past us, toward pioneers trading with Indians.

I wondered where the elder fathers were like Benjamin Franklin, John Adams, George Washington, Thomas Jefferson. Those I could relate to. Although what had I founded lately? "What about Phillip?"

"I leave boy with you. If that okay." She kissed me softly on my cheek.

I could see our reflections on the glass. Martine had her eyes closed. "Okay. But how long?" I asked.

"I no know."

"This doesn't sound good, Martine. I'm worried about you. Where are you going?"

"I go home, Jimmy. To island. Come back soon." She took my hand again.

We stopped in front of a bear attacking settlers near their flimsy houses. A long painted road with green trees spread out over a small piece of land that disappeared at the far edge of the diorama. One of the women settlers had thrown her hand over her mouth, and another had buried her face in her elbow. They were frozen in time, frozen in their fear forever.

"When you come back let's get married." It wasn't very romantic. We were in front of wolves eyeing two fawns. Plastic trees and bushes, and paper-mache rocks protected them as if we were gods, able to see everything yet unable to do anything. I took both of her hands into mine.

"Yes, Jimmy. Soon I divorced." She smiled. Phillip ran to her side.

When she did leave it seemed as if Martine was gone for a long time although it was only three weeks. Phillip and I kept busy. I remembered once being as young as Phillip and how adult problems seemed burdensome while all I wanted to do was to follow a bird that whistled in a funny way or to invent something that went terribly wrong and destroyed most of the neighborhood. Martine and I were two translations and each was right. I missed her. Phillip did too.

"More nut," Phillip said the first morning about his school peanut butter and jelly sandwich. "Martine put more nut on."

I thought a lot about Martine's absence, my fingers twitching with caffeine, a book about someone else's journey to an island falling out of my hands. There was too much stillness for a young boy and an old man alone together. I liked looking into Phillip's face and seeing Martine there. It was a lot of work cooking, making the boy do homework, getting him to school on time, and cleaning. Phillip's life at school settled down to sometimes getting kicked into the dirt in the yard or pushed into a sidewalk. I tried to help him by giving him the advice I thought Martine would. But by the third week I was tired, and I was younger then. In some ways Aaron was easier.

When Martine returned, she cried on my shoulders after Phillip was asleep. "It no work, Jimmy. I no get divorce." I never really understood why.

***

Emily and I struggled with the wheelchair, its machinery heavy and rambling, and the wheels continuously caught on floor irregularities, furniture, and people. This time I did dress up the boy, a cap, a thin jacket, sunglasses. Just another boy. Emily wore a wig, dark clothes, make-up. I tried to disguise myself to look like everyone else, an old suit, a hat pulled down onto my forehead. I watched the boy moving his head all around in order to take everything in, his fingers clutching the arm rests, grasping and ungrasping.

I wondered what went on inside his mind as we painstakingly bumped him down the apartment stairs, out onto the street with all its comings and goings, and then into the familiar subway station with its pools of specific light. Aaron sniffed the various geographies of air as if he was sorting, labeling different parts of the city that people brought along with them. Dampness fell out of the dark there. Several birds dived at us, confessing their intentions as they missed our bodies, landing high in the ceiling. The boy held his palms over his ears and I realized that the noise was probably intolerable for him. Too many conversations, the roar of the trains, people jostling one another. Aaron opened his mouth and if he could have screamed, maybe he would have.

I saw two missionaries in a corner talking to a teenager whose bursts of orange hair swam over his face. He pocketed the brochures and tried to move away but the man in black and white, with a ponytail, caught him by the arm, said something else. I pulled my hat tightly around my forehead and looked away.

Emily, Aaron, and I hurried onto a subway train, the wheelchair whirring, jiggling at the threshold. We huddled in a corner until we reached our stop. The exit was above ground and we took an elevator down onto the street. The boy finally took his hands off of his ears. I checked the address and we walked a few blocks. Rosemary would probably be angry about Aaron and maybe I wanted her to be angry. I was tired of women vanishing.

At the address I was given, a historical, ornate apartment building loomed. Stone replicas of winged beasts studded the upper floors, ivy braided small iron balconies halfway up, and stained glass windows lined the bottom floor. A small, fenced yard sat on the side with a carved stone fountain. Gray squirrels sifted through leaves and the sparse grass under a bench. I imagined peace and quiet within large, empirical rooms filled with solidly built antique furniture. I told the doorman who we wanted to visit. Rosemary. At first he seemed perplexed. But when I described her he nodded and rang up a number.

"Quite a group to see you." Then he pointed to the elevators.

The boy was silently beside himself with all the new experiences as a uniformed man lifted the elevator to the correct floor. The boy moved the small bits of himself that he could move, his wrists circling around themselves, his neck straining, his head turning every which way. Emily resembled some strange child's idea of a grown-up. I had a hidden quality, like some ancient detective. I wasn't sure who Rosemary would be angrier about, Aaron, Emily, or me.

I rang a doorbell encircled with metal scroll. The same doctor who tended to Aaron answered the door in the same dark suit, his white hair shorn close to his scalp, eyeglasses perched on his nose as he looked us over. He sighed deeply when he saw the boy. He opened the door wider and Rosemary came to the threshold dressed in black with her braids tucked into the back of her head in a bun. I expected to see elegant furniture against simple windows, but all I saw was black draped everywhere and gibberish scribbled on all the mirrors.

"Come in," Rosemary said to us. "Thank you," she said to the doctor, "you can go now. I can handle this." The man grabbed his bag sitting by the door, and left, wordlessly.

When I sold tickets, I had always known what I was supposed to do, and I did it. Even when crazy people called me names because trains didn't go where they wanted them to go, or they didn't have money, or they had nothing better to do. But once I retired, I could take things more personally. I could do things I wasn't supposed to do. Sometimes I wanted to see how it felt.

"This place is enormous." Emily twirled round and round the gothic apartment with black, hulking shapes, her wig askew. "I like what you've done with it."

"I knew you'd be trouble," Rosemary answered. "And you," she said, pointing at me, "how could you do this to the boy after all I've told you?"

"You haven't told me anything."

Then Rosemary began crying large, fat tears, rolling unashamedly down her cheeks, which was something I didn't expect. I was stunned.

"Sit down." Rosemary sat in a carved wooden chair with black cloth on the back.

Emily and I wheeled the boy to the side and sat on a sofa covered with black chiffon.

Rosemary brought out a handkerchief. "Things aren't always about you." She was looking at me. She began crying again. "My mother died this morning. I miss her terribly already." She wiped away some tears. "I wanted to give all our money to THEM for a while, but she didn't want me to. It was her money after all. But now I can give my portion of it to whomever I want." She smiled. "I guess there's a bit of a silver lining." Then she started crying again.

I was speechless. The boy held out his hands. I gave him paper and a pen. He began to write *a fool and...* but I snatched the writing implements out of his hands. He started coughing soundlessly. I wondered how much he knew. He had spent a lot of time overhearing people and their foibles, but he hadn't spent enough time around them, making his own mistakes.

I patted Rosemary's hand while Emily inspected the room, maybe searching for secrets. We were a strange, little group. I noticed the boy's eye sockets seemed deeper once I removed his sunglasses and his cap. His face was narrower, not as puffy. He was thinner, taller. He was growing.

"And you brought Aaron here. Good God, what were you thinking, Jimmy?" Rosemary wailed, making her crying piercing. The folds of her black dress gathered tears.

I touched the boy's dark hair for the first time without needing to do anything to it. It felt like fur. "The boy needs to get out, see things for himself. Well, you know what I mean." I tried to make my gesture seem generous. I had actually wanted to make her as mad as I was. Only I wasn't angry anymore. At my age everything dissipated fairly quickly.

"God knows what will happen." Rosemary shook her head, the last of her tears flying around her face, some strands of gray hair loosening, clinging to her neck. "Well, you're the only one stupid or crazy or brave enough to find out. Is any part of him bleeding?"

"I don't think so." I felt kind of bad.

"Why? Why did you do it?" She stopped crying at least.

"I think I see too much of myself in him." The boy had a wisp of a smile on his lips. Emily was peeking under some black fabric over a desk and trying to surreptitiously pull out some drawers. The boy held out his hands and I gave him the paper and pen.

Rosemary spit out, "And what do you think he's like?"

"Shy and devilishly handsome."

"He's innocent and needy. Nothing at all like you."

Every story has rooms that are too small and families that try to live in them.

"Anyway, we should get Aaron back." Rosemary began searching the boy for hidden bleeding. The boy blinked over and over.

"I wasn't sure that I would ever see you again," I told her.

Rosemary just shook her head, closed her eyes for a moment. She looked over at Emily. "Did you find anything of interest over there, Emily?"

Emily pushed a drawer back in and turned around quickly, looking guilty.

"That's my mother's silverware drawer. What are you looking for?" Rosemary looked at me.

"I can't take either of them anywhere."

"Secrets," Emily whispered and sat on the black sofa.

"And?" Rosemary asked.

Emily lifted her empty hands. "Nothing yet."

"And what has Aaron gotten out of this trip?" Rosemary looked at me again.

The boy wrote, *I'm coming into my own.*

"I'm sorry," I said. "I wanted to tell you about an ad I saw for acrobatic training." I explained the little I knew about the school, the little I had seen in the subway ad. I had called the school and explained Aaron's vast limitations to them. They said they would try and do something with him if we signed a liability paper. It was more than I had hoped. "It could help him get physically stronger."

The boy blinked again and again. *I want.*

Emily said, "Hmm, that sounds fascinating. Flying through the air, somersaulting with almost nothing to hold on to."

"I don't have the money," I said.

"They won't go for it. What could you be thinking?" Rosemary was agitated. "They'll be angry enough about this as it is."

I took Rosemary's hand and she didn't pull it away. "We don't have to tell THEM. It's about taking a chance."

***

Don and Bill were shaking off their raincoats inside the diner and water fell spasmodically everywhere. The waitress ran past them quickly so she wouldn't get wet. Thunder outside punctured our thoughts. I liked how the city gleamed and became slippery. Cars and buses sliced through the water making waves and pools that closed behind them. Emily and I had to watch for everything on our way there, cars, people, and umbrellas so nothing suspect would inadvertently happen to us. Car lights shone into our faces as though we had done something illegal. I wanted us both to remain in one piece.

"Where's Jack?" I asked.

"Here," he bellowed as he made his way to the table on crutches. Jack had stitches crisscrossing his rugged jaw. "This is what trying to outrace a car does to you. I had just stepped off a sidewalk and bam. I really didn't even know what hit me." He balanced on one crutch and patted the top of Emily's head with his hand. "Good to see you, little girl." Then he slid into a booth.

Emily put her fists on her waist. "I'm hardly a little girl. I'm probably more woman than some of your dates."

"She's got you there," Bill said.

"Yeah, some of his prospects only talk to Jack on Sundays since it's the one day he doesn't drink. It's no use trying to talk to him the rest of the week," Don said. "I'm surprised it wasn't one of them that punched his lights out. Maybe he only thought it was a car that hit him."

"I think I'd notice the difference," Jack said, sulking.

"Good to see you, Emily. We old farts missed you," Bill said. "We don't have much family of our own."

"Except each other," I added. Jack patted my scruffy head.

"So how's it going with that boyfriend, Hammer?" Don inquired.

Emily made a face. "What a jerk. He dumped me for a cheerleader and acts like he hardly ever even knew me. Nobody talks to me at school. I give up on school anyway. There's nothing for me there."

Bill held his hands over his ears like the boy, Aaron, did. Bill said, "I don't want to hear it. I wish your mother would make you go."

"She doesn't care. She didn't make it through high school anyway," Emily said.

The waitress flew over to Emily with a hamburger and soda before the rest of us had ordered. "Here, honey, some guy said it wasn't what he ordered. And the soda's on the house."

Emily smiled. "It's better than home here."

Our waitress grinned proudly.

***

Rosemary wanted me to go to another meeting. She was there somewhere although we pretended that we hardly knew each other. I watched for active gray braids. Many people were in black pants and white tee shirts although THEM seemed to be relaxing about some of their rules. Why, I didn't know. The lecture was "The Danger in Making Plans." "What We're Up Against" and "How to Live Now" were upcoming. I clutched the programs, sipped coffee, wondering, as many people did before me, what it meant to be human. Was caring about someone enough? Using tools? Having too many memories? Language? What did that make the boy? We were waiting for Brian, who was now using disguises when he went places, afraid to be himself anymore, afraid someone might have a gun. A black man with white hair approached me. He was about my age, had a neat beard and wore some kind of a white scarf that reminded me of a napkin, tucked into his black tee shirt.

He held out a veined hand to shake mine, "You're the one with Aaron. My name's Harold."

I knew Brian couldn't create such a good disguise. I shook his hand. "My name's Jimmy." I looked around, caught sight of some gray hair, but it was loose and shoulder-length. "So what did THEM live like in the old days? What's your history? Were you shunned by some country or religion? What made it start? What attracts you to this group?"

"You don't ask many questions, do you?" He laughed. "Brian was the one that discovered his relationship to something like God. He's interested in broadening our boundaries through suffering, giving, and acceptance." He laughed again good-naturedly. "So we're relatively new. He believes that we discover what's unique about us as individuals through those activities. So he's kind of old Testament. I especially like the idea that our spirits or souls can move from body to body as we reach certain levels of spirituality and that the soul is found in the dark spaces between our molecules. It means, of course, that Aaron can abandon his body when he's ready. Also, we are all connected to one another. There are parts of everyone within each of us. THEM," he nodded, "Theological Human Evolvement Movement."

"Thanks. I was hoping for another perspective."

"I think Brian was inspired. I like feeling that I'm spiritually progressing, and it feels so outwardly visible."

"We're so invisible. As older people, I mean." It suddenly hit me. "Do you think that we, too, want other better bodies?"

"What for?" Harold asked. "So we can pick up women

or run a marathon or something? Who's to say what body we'd get."

"Just to be treated differently. We could have a whole other lifetime to fix the mistakes we already spent this lifetime making."

Harold's pale brown eyes turned toward the floor. "Who's to say that everything wouldn't turn out the same way in another life. You have to accept Fate or God. Things are better than that, especially here, with these people. They understand. We work to spread the ideas of suffering, giving, acceptance."

What if Rosemary and I progressed so rapidly that we could switch bodies? I didn't want to think about that. It was the intention underneath it all that mattered to me but I didn't know what mine was. "What about the Great Event, the one they've been talking about?"

"I don't know anything about that. There's a governing group that knows stuff like that." He stuffed his hands into his pants pockets.

"Doesn't something like that worry you?'

Harold's head moved from side to side. "Naw, I know they'll take care of me. You too."

Sometimes it was like talking to a wall, a wall that reminded me of myself when I didn't question concepts or argue, which was rare. I closed my eyes. I thought about seeing Brian's God, asking Him to tell me how things were and what was going to happen. It was like listening to the wind blowing through trees, or a ghost trying to tell me something with its hands. When I opened my eyes a middle-aged man with a blonde beard and mustache, thick glasses, and a hat tilted low onto his forehead was standing in front of me with Rosemary. Harold had left. The man removed his beard and mustache and hat and handed them all to Rosemary. I briefly thought of a city where everyone wore disguises and therefore no one recognized one another.

Brian said, "So you think you know everything, Jimmy? You believe that you know what's best for others?" He looked stern.

"No, of course not. But you have to cut down the trees sometimes in order to see the sky."

"You can chase a blue ball or keep it in your hands and hold onto it forever," Brian said, smiling, reminding me of the boy for a moment.

"What harm will it do the boy to try something new?" I inquired. Rosemary wasn't helping me. She was silent.

"Aaron has the ear of God. But you might be right. There's another boy we've been cultivating. Not much has come from Aaron. Look what I'm reduced to now." Brian held up his limp, hairy disguise. "Of course, anyone who has something important to say risks being killed." He placed the empty hat and twitching hair back into Rosemary's hands. Rosemary coddled it. "What do you think, Rosemary?"

But she didn't say anything. She just nodded. She was wordless before Brian.

"You need to find a way to pay for these acrobatic lessons yourself. We'll be cutting down on helping you too.

Right now I need to concentrate on trying to stay alive. Are you sure you want to keep the boy?" Brian's eyebrows rose into triangles. "You are a bit of a loner."

"The boy is more alone than I am."

"Everyone is disabled in some way," Brian answered. He shrugged his shoulders. "I'm burdened by my beliefs and opinions, according to the rest of the world." He looked at me.

"I respect my own doubt." I didn't want people to tell me how to live. I looked at Rosemary. "And I want to help those I care about."

"And, naturally, to help yourself. Why are you here?"

"I like the exchange of ideas."

Brian nodded. "Good. Good. I need to go now."

He and Rosemary rose to the stage without disguises. Brian stood behind the podium. "Although today's lecture is 'The Danger of Making Plans' I wanted to tell you about one of my own plans." He smiled at Rosemary, who stood quietly by his side. "Rosemary and I will be married soon..."

I stood without thinking and left, my body eventually following me.

PART II

Chapter Eleven, Carly

"I don't know what you're doing. I don't know you," I screamed at myself. There was nothing left inside. I was empty. I whirled around. My stomach burned. I wrapped myself in coats, hats, gloves. I unbuttoned a coat, fanned my waist. My hands moved by themselves sometimes, fixing stuff. I hurt.

I was hungry so I went to one of the places with too much food. It was early in the morning and there was something left inside the large garbage bins under the lights that wanted to grab me and turn me around. There were no Things out yet. I smelled the dead: old shoes; parts of tiny meat bodies; blood; silence; and green that had already turned brown. I ate thinking of napkins and gardens and animals running through a village. I felt safe with the weight and shape of the ghost-maker poking at me through my clothes.

I argued with myself. It was never-ending. "I want stairs, not a TV that plays with my eyes." "In the shelter they reach into my ears and try to send me messages." "The devices at hospitals are so that people aren't lonely." I was whispering. Air touched me impersonally again so I bit it. But I was full. Things were starting to walk by in their work clothes and driving their stories on wheels. I looked longingly at the rows of beautiful, empty carts but none of them called to me. I petted them. Some wheels turned. There was nothing to them.

Then I saw it, behind an old, rusting car in the corner of

the parking lot, a lamp light still bearing down hard on it, a beautiful, mangled shopping cart with some ribs missing. I ran to it. The wheels were intact but sad, a wet cardboard box lay inside. Was it for me? When I opened it I found an armless plastic doll. I didn't like her eyes and her tangled hair. She said mean words and snapped stiff lips at me. I threw her into the bushes.

"I want to make things grow," I whispered to my new cart. I nodded my head, smiled, lay my gloved hand along the steel basket. We were careful with one another. This was a start.

"I'll fill you up," I said. For now the cart was shy.

I pushed it past the road full of loose cars, near a woman with cerebral red hair, under the curious gray sky with its bulky clouds. I saw a policeman playing with traffic but he didn't have any expression when I walked by, pushing my new companion.

"The first treasure is the most important," I whispered into the handlebar. I saw a mirror like an eye, fake flowers, crosses sleeping by the side of the road. Maybe the tambourine or pictures and pages of music. I picked up the tambourine but it sounded like trees falling so I put it back. The written music was made of freckles and it was quiet so I placed that in the small basket.

"See what I can do for you," I murmured. "Music."

Then the cart began shaking convulsively. I had done that myself once or twice. It wasn't laughter. Metal clanged. When I looked up, a friend who drank too much tried to smile at me with half of her face, her stringy hair whipping anyone nearby. Her hand slapped the edges of my new companion like a fish. She wore men's clothes and smelled bad. Her men's shoes were untied and the laces dripped onto the sidewalk.

"I heard you did something stupid." She was coughing.

"I was looking at things the way they truly were."

She was so thin I could push my hands right through her. Her hair was growing old.

"You know you're going to get into trouble." Her hands left my cart and her body rocked back and forth as if there was a strong wind. "You should give it to me." She held out one bony hand.

"I know what you're doing." My new cart was between us.

"Okay," she said. "But if you need someplace to stay I heard Brian is building a new place off of tenth street and it should be ready soon."

I made a face. I didn't like his name. I spit. "He eats my brain."

She turned her back to go. "I heard it's nice and the food's going to be good."

Chapter Twelve, Jimmy

There were too many things wrong with me. I couldn't take care of myself so I couldn't care for the boy. I wasn't exactly perfect romantic material, too old, my disobedient hair was falling out, and my legs were stringy. I was argumentative, a coward, and riddled with scars. I wasn't wealthy. I wasn't charming. I was too independent and self-contained. I listened to the subway gliding by like a noisy river. It was a background for my uncomfortable thoughts. Fluorescent lights targeted random people and I wondered about their lives, whether they had good relationships, families, homes, money. Somehow it was soothing, abstractly comparing and contrasting. Then someone patted my arm. I jumped from my seat at the touch, sat down again.

"Are you going to be sick?" A young woman hovered over me, her brown eyebrows contracting. She wore an evening dress and boots. The way people dressed was the only way I knew whether it was day or night in the subway station.

"No." I was bent over my bench. My stomach was rolled up into a little ball. I cupped my head in my hands and wanted to say, *Love me. Stay with me.* I said, "Thank you for asking."

She sat down. "Are you sure? You don't look well."

A train was jostling our hair, stapling our clothes to our

bodies. There was a moment of loudness and then a lot of silence. How could Rosemary marry Brian? Did she choose him? Or did he choose her? Force her? Did he have other wives (as was rumored)? Was it that kind of religion? I hadn't researched Brian's personal life. I should have. I had been too comfortable, trusted them too easily in my own pugnacious way, lulled by all the talking. My life drifted into my throat and was stuck there.

"I should call somebody." She snaked one arm around my shoulders.

I hadn't been touched so casually since kissing Rosemary. "No, I'm fine. It was just something I did. You know how those things come back to haunt you later on?" I sat up straighter.

"Unfortunately, I do." The woman laughed like paper crumpling. She patted my back. "Those existential crises can really kick you in the ass. Or maybe in your case, in the stomach." She stood up. "Well then, there's nothing a doctor can do." She took a few steps forward and got on the next train that came by and was out of my life.

I wanted to ask Martine for advice. But she and Phillip were gone. It had all been my fault. Maybe Brian was right, the boy was too much responsibility. Maybe I didn't deserve Rosemary. I sat with my head in my hands for a while. Then I rose to go home in the inviolate darkness to the boy who would be sleeping or feigning sleep.

***

The next morning I wasn't surprised when Rosemary didn't arrive to help with Aaron. An elderly woman came who resembled a witch from some fairy tale like Hansel and Gretel. She had a long nose, wispy gray hair, a crackling voice, and sticks that were called arms and legs. There was no way she could lift the boy so both of us struggled to get him to his bath, even using the hidden wheelchair.

The whole time she chided me, "Did you think you had something going with Rosemary? Is that why you ran out of the meeting the other night? An old man like you? What could you be thinking? Compare yourself to Brian." She sounded like my conscience but with a shrill, dry voice. I didn't have time to answer before she continued, "Sure, Brian is attractive to women and he does already have several children and the women that go with them, but he also picked Rosemary for other reasons since she's too old to have children."

"What do you think they are?"

"How should I know? Do I look like I read minds?" She seemed to be in a foul humor. It must have been because she was chasing all those little children on her broomstick, trying to eat some. "Didn't you notice the ring that appeared on her engagement finger, or are you blind too?"

Guilty as charged. Both she and Rosemary were right. I didn't notice much.

But the boy waved his arms as we were moving him into the bathtub. He wrote *Sometimes there are too many wrong ideas, other times too few.*

Lately he had an opinion about everything. Before his

bath one morning he wrote *Don't like alphabet of the water.* As if the water was talking to him or writing him. Often I didn't understand him. His English and writing skills were excellent now. From our lessons? I could finally enter his mind. It was much more complicated there than I had imagined.

When the woman and I both stared at him he wrote *Maybe I can escape the story that's held together by two unlikely people.* We were in the bathroom. I took his notebook away. He didn't always make sense.

"No Mister," the woman was scrubbing him hard, "you don't get to escape anything, especially me." She actually cackled. "And do you think you're so special, Aaron? Well you better get over that. There are three others like you that want to take your place. So no, you won't be getting the service you got before. Did you think you were the only one? You'll be stuck with me. Rosemary's busy now and I don't know when she'll be back here." She looked at me and her long nose peeked through her ropey gray strands of hair. Her hands were sunk into the tub, vigorously washing Aaron's limbs. Bubbles formed and popped quickly. She had once probably been pretty. Now she wore rubber bands in a clump on her right wrist and what resembled garlic swung around her neck on a string. I didn't want to ask why. "So you boys will be on your own and free to do what you what. I have some tips for you if you want." But she was engrossed with taking care of the boy and stopped talking.

Things were changing, and I didn't know what to make of it all. I had been able to put the boy into the background for a while, but then he resurfaced, his needs became overwhelming again. "Hey," I told the woman, "I have some friends who'd probably like to meet you. We eat at a diner."

"I don't need any more friends," she answered. The boy was done.

We laboriously moved him back to his bed. "What about Rosemary?"

She was searching for her black bag. One skinny arm shot out and circled its handle. "Want my advice? Go do something about it."

I nodded. Pigeons the color of ash made a commotion at my kitchen window. Their wings flew up into the air. Maybe there was a speck of food out there.

She laughed again, a high-pitched noise. "It's too late to escape. For the both of you."

"Escape what?"

"You should ask Rosemary."

I opened the door for her. I couldn't wait for her to leave.

***

I wondered what Martine had made of all my friends at the diner. She hadn't come often and she didn't say anything about them. Don, Jack, and Bill had invited her one winter day on her birthday. It was odd to see Martine without Phillip. Martine's mahogany hair was loose around her shoulders and she wore a simple, ironed dress with flat shoes and a heavy coat that she held wrapped tightly around her body, even when she sat down. Martine found cold weather tortuous. "Inside me head I freeze. No can think."

"Some of our thoughts weren't that fluid to begin with," Bill commented after everyone had been introduced. Everyone wished Martine a good birthday.

"It good in America. Jimmy work in station. Things big in America. Safe," Martine said, unfolding her napkin then making a bird shape out of it on her lap.

I wondered if innocence really existed in adults or whether knowledge was being gathered. Even then I knew that the world would come to her in one form or another as it always did.

"You haven't lived here long, have you?" Jack asked.

Martine shook her dark, glossy hair.

"The longer you live here the more you'll like it. There's lots to do and see. You'll get used to the cold. Hey, by the time you get used to it, it'll be getting hot here again." The always optimistic Bill.

"Seasons." Martine said all the word's syllables. "So many clothes. Always changing." She shook her head again.

Another waitress sauntered by, who looked too bloated for her uniform. Her hair was teased into an auburn bird perched on top of her head. She pulled out a pad from a pocket on her apron and a pencil that had been hidden in the hair over her ear. "What would you like?"

"Something you don't have here," Don commented.

"Try me," the waitress retorted. "I'll start with you." She looked at Martine.

"Warm. Warm food."

"Umm, soup, coffee?" the waitress offered.

Martine nodded, not asking anything more like what kind of soup? Everyone else ordered specific meals from the menu. Martine could read only basic English, not everything. She had lasted four months in her marriage with the American man she had met in the islands. They had married there before he brought her here. She was alarmed at his sudden bursts of violence when she first arrived in America.

I couldn't tell whether Martine was embarrassed, shy, or didn't really care what she ate. She preferred her island food, oxtail, okra, plantains, strange and wondrous fruit. Maybe she wanted to try something new. I was proud of her.

Don, Jack, and Bill were shy too, ordering extra napkins, trying to make sure she was comfortable. "Sugar or salt?" one of them asked her.

"Tell me about life on the island," Don asked, even then beginning to think about a way to change his life.

Martine told him about coconuts, mangos, melons, fish, and how delicious their scrap and bones were in a soup, about the shabby houses that allowed any breeze to sweep through all their meager possessions, giving them a fresh, new scent. She talked about how sleepy and slow life was there, what it was like to see your family every day and knowing everyone and their business in your town. She described the sun removing its robe. How in the dense, tropical forests there were sounds underneath and over the sounds you heard. How if you fell asleep too long in those forests vegetation would grow over you. She spoke for a long time in her special English. Don, Jack, and Bill seemed interested. We ate. Then she cried at her memories, pulling her coat closer around her. My embarrassed friends didn't know what to do. Jack and Bill were suddenly interested in their empty plates and Don looked out the window. One by one they all went back to work.

***

I ran into Emily at the grocery store. She was browsing through detergents and potato chips. She seemed to be taking her time, doing everything in slow motion. I watched her for a little while before I said hello. I had just passed through the polite stomach aids, towards the helpful pain relievers. I recognized her unmistakable ears, thin nose, the wild black hair. Her elongated limbs were sprawled in all directions over the plastic bags and boxes. She was holding some cans in a basket.

"Dinner tonight," she claimed, holding up a can of franks and beans.

"I've lost Rosemary."

"Hmm," she said. "Is that a bad thing?"

"Yes, at my age it is. I don't get a lot of chances. I thought that nothing could hurt me anymore."

"Okay, what happened?" She sounded a little exasperated.

I told her about the meeting and Brian while we walked leisurely back to our building.

"I didn't know you belonged to a cult."

"You better be careful or we'll kidnap you in the middle of the night and do weird things to you." With Emily I could joke about things.

"Do you promise? I'm more bored at home than at school. There's stuff happening at home but it's the same old stuff."

"You're not in school?"

"No. But I do have some advice for you that a friend at school gave me about Hammer." She hesitated. "If you're crazy about her, fight for her." We were at my front door. "I guess Hammer didn't mean that much to me because I sure didn't fight for him." She turned and went up the stairs to her apartment.

I was getting advice from high school girls. I could hear her mother say out her door, "Where's that girl with our dinner? I swear I heard her voice on the stairs. We're hungry here. Hey, you're pretty good-looking for a kid. What'd you say your name was? A nail or wrench or something." She laughed, the loud noise spiraling down the stairwell. "Hammer? Wasn't that it?"

***

The boy was clean. I propped him up in his bed, gave him pen and paper. It was impossible to tell what time of day it was in his room. There wasn't a window. What about a city full of disabled people? Would anything ever get done?

"You're such a part of my life now. I forget you're here,

especially when you're sleeping or quiet." I was nostalgic about him while he was still there.

My choices are flaccid.

"Your language use is wonderfully interesting." Unless he meant something else. "One of us should have some happiness at least briefly in this diminished world." Aaron's eyes appeared clotted, latched with something slick that I would have to clean off.

Find Rosemary's seams, what holds her together.

"Brian already has." I averted my eyes from his vegetable body.

My body is chewed but my mind isn't. What about yours?

What was he implying? My mind? Or my body? How did he know I was thinking about his body? We, both of us, were afraid of our bodies and the myriad ways they would fail us. We had that in common. But he had an unassailable circuitry. I couldn't predict what he would say.

Both he and Emily were saying I had to do something. They were probably right. I peered through the open door of the bedroom and out the kitchen window. A pigeon shuffled along the outside sill, pale and bleary as a television screen full of static. Oddly shaped, rectangular buildings stood upright in rows behind the bird.

"I'm not sure I know her well enough to do the right thing," I finally answered him.

I'm learning to become my own father.

"I need to manufacture my own love. Then I need to project Rosemary within it."

The boy blinked once. *Yes.* He wrote, *But there's only so much we can do.*

"I've been saying that all along." We? He understood a lot without having experienced any of it. A part of me wanted to save him and another part still wanted to leave him somewhere. "I need to talk to her."

Brian is too large.

"Do you know him well?"

Two blinks.

Brian could be his father. The margin of the boy's flesh was disappearing. "You're growing taller and thinner."

Maybe I'll stop eating and drinking now.

"No, please don't. I'll take you outside. We can start that circus class. You can fly."

The boy jerked, mewled. Maybe it was an attempted laugh. I didn't know what to do with him, or what to do about Rosemary either. Aaron wanted pliant walls, new landscapes, egregious parents. I assumed he wanted to be consolable like the rest of us, but maybe I was wrong. Maybe he wanted something different all together. "What would you like to do?"

Want to be kissed. (Not by you).

"At least that's something." Although who would kiss him?

He knotted his fingers and threw them around. His body unribboned itself, trying to fling his bones out toward his skin. Then his fingers settled beside his legs, which were hidden under a blanket. He wrote, *I could pour myself into somebody else.*

"What about your mother?"

A rain-soaked woman crying. I don't remember who.

"Any brothers or sisters?"

Two blinks. *My imagination.*

"Soon," I said. But there wasn't any question.

***

Rosemary telephoned.

"I didn't know you could make yourself so distant," I told her.

Then she came to my apartment, appearing tall beside me. She stooped, placing her bag for the boy on my floor while making sharp, little movements with her arms.

"I suppose I need to explain myself," Rosemary stated, her familiar, gray braids flinging themselves at her shoulders. She wore shoes with small heels and a dress that looked torn at the hem. I noticed the big diamond ring that rotated down, underneath her finger, from gravity.

My heart was racing. "I want a chance."

"For what? It feels like there's nothing left of me." Rosemary sat on my sofa, deflated. Her dress pounced on her calves. "THEM is all I have left. At least I can help with something there. There will be lots of changes."

I sat down next to her. "You must tell me about that." I kissed her softly, lips against lips, as though I was whispering. She didn't pull away immediately.

"You don't even know me," she protested. Her hand was between us. She was breathing as though she meant it.

"I like complex board games or cards, watching trains, reading books, life's mysteries, subway tunnels, disabled young boys I have to take care of, and evening because it sweeps the old out and ushers the new in," I told her. "I like my friends."

She crossed her hands on her lap. "Okay," she said, "I like ornate, gold objects I can hold in my hands, prayers for everything, THEM, work that makes you tired at the end of the day, and sick young boys somebody else helps take care of." She finally smiled.

"Maybe we should start all over again," I offered. "From the beginning."

"I don't know," she looked at her fingers as though she was reading a newspaper, "behind desire lurks destruction."

"I couldn't have said it better."

"There's Brian." She held up her ring, which sparkled in my dimly lit room as though it was happy to be free from the earth. "It's not as if he would miss me. It was as much my idea as his."

"Why?" I was getting tired of asking because I couldn't get a satisfactory answer.

"I need to pretend to have a life of my own. There's mother's inherited money..."

I took her hand, feeling the small veins in her wrist, her soft skin becoming slack and overlapping. She was growing calcareous and I wanted to burrow into her because she was another piece of me that had broken off long ago and lived separately and differently.

"..and this marriage was decided a while ago. Before you."

"We both need to reshape our spaces. We've been stationary while the earth's been moving around us. Cancel the coming marriage." I nibbled at her neck with its curlicues of gray hair but this time she moved away.

"We're both too old for this."

***

"So," Emily said, hesitating at the top of the peeling apartment stairs, "Aaron told me that you and Rosemary are getting it on."

"That's not quite accurate. She's mulling it over, but I'm hopeful."

"Hope means you're not where you want to be. That's what Aaron always says."

"Have you been talking to the boy behind my back?"

She came down the stairs in a solicitous manner. "He IS the only person who'll listen to me and not judge me."

"You're starting to sound like us old geezers."

"Or a person with disabilities, or a person who's tired of what everybody else wants." Her sharp little face looked sad.

"What's the matter, Emily?"

"What's not the matter?"

"We're all cranky for different reasons but sometimes our problems meet in a dark alley and conspire with one another and maybe something good will come out of it all. Do you want to go to the diner with me today?"

"Oh, Jimmy, I do like it there but not today. I want to

do something different. We're too far from the sea, any sea. You know I saw one when I was a baby. At least that's what my mother told me. And it's springtime."

"Come on, Emily. We won't abandon each other."

"That's what they all say." She turned, rubbed her neck the way a cat washes itself before it's ready to jump away.

Her arms were the color of wet earth in the fading light of the stairway. "You'll find someone. You're still young and have plenty of time. You're a beautiful girl. Any boy would be lucky to have you. You'll see." I was becoming everyone's father. The job seemed to consist of mollifying people. "Did you talk to Aaron when I wasn't there, maybe when one of the caregivers was there?"

She nodded, turning back toward me.

"What else did the boy say?"

"Just what you said. That I'm beautiful."

"Be careful."

"Of what? He's the one person that I don't think could hurt me."

"You might be surprised." I sounded like Rosemary.

"He said that the end is starting."

"What did he mean?"

"He didn't tell me and I didn't have a chance to ask him before I was rushed out."

"Of course, that's always true. The end is always moving closer."

"Whatever you say, Jimmy." Emily flipped her dark hair and lowered her darker sunglasses onto her nose. "I am looking forward to those lessons. But for now I want to catch a few subway trains to the sea. It isn't the nicest beach and ocean around, but it'll have to do for now."

"Yes," I said, "I know what you mean."

CARLY, CHAPTER THIRTEEN

Suddenly I was on the sidewalk, blood splashed onto my new shopping cart, and a red bubble was spreading beneath me from somewhere. Blue lined the inside of my closed eyelids so I screamed and screamed. I watched TV inside of my eyes. Shapes beckoned, then pushed me away. The blue was there.

Things arrived in a loud, whirring vehicle. I couldn't tell if they were dead or not. Sky crawled out from behind them to take a look at me and then it shriveled away again.

"Don't move me until I tell you my secret," I told them. But their hands were on me searching for the place that was open and hurt.

They were talking to each other, ignoring me.

"Where's she bleeding from?" one asked the other.

"I can't tell with all these clothes," a woman in ruined green pants answered, rummaging through parts of my body. "Does this hurt?"

She pressed my stomach and I saw stars fleeing. The stars were writing with a weird light on my cart. I concentrated on my wrists. Then crows began catching the stars all around me in their beaks, swallowing. I could taste metal and bile and I tried to stop screaming. I said, "I'm not sick anymore."

"Yes, you are, dear." She puffed the words out like curtains. "And there's help for it."

"I don't want the crows to watch me."

She signaled them to begin. Men came, poured over me, and lifted me into the car that started to shriek again. There was no air in there and they attached tubes to me like questions.

"I know what you're doing."

"Then you know we're doing this for your own good." The woman in green looked at one of the men. She rolled her eyes, said, "I want a cigarette really badly right now."

I lifted my head. I watched my despairing cart grow smaller and smaller in the distance through the tiny back window. I cupped my ears with my bloody hands. The woman put something in one of the tubes snaking into my body.

"Don't touch my legs or boots," I said. I was getting sleepy. I could feel my pistol inside a thick sock, under the boot back, so the Things wouldn't find it. Crows were eating my lips, pecking at my eyes. I brushed them away.

"I don't think we'll need to, dear." The green woman's head tilted toward me and then away. "She's the third one from the street today," she told one of the men.

Crows were falling out of the air around her. They were crashing on the floor. I couldn't open my mouth, warn her about anything.

One of the men asked the green woman, "So do you think I should talk to my girlfriend and tell her how I really feel? She works in a bowling alley, you know." His words floated around the car and then out a window.

"I don't know. I'm exhausted," the woman said, moving her hands over my eyes.

Crows gathered around me, lifted me in their wings. One nudged the ghost-maker. "It's mine," I wanted to say, but I couldn't. I wanted to move my arms and legs, but I couldn't. We were flying around and around in a circle inside the car. All those dark feathers. The birds were hungry for me, balancing me in the center of their flock. We were going to crash through the back door. I wanted to ask, "Where are we going?" but I couldn't.

***

I woke up in white. There was no color, no sound. Windows full of rain. Dead Things around me. I bolted upright from the softness. "Where are the fucking crows?" I screamed, starting to rip out the tubes that were invading my arms. I felt too much foreign stuff inside my body. Light was burning me to a crisp. The floor was all milk. Moths fluttered inside my head.

"I need a chair like a rocket. I need more frost here," I whispered. I saw my clothes in a large, brown saucy pile by my bed. I peeled off sheets, a nice blanket I would keep if I had my cart. My boots were still on, the flaps open, laces around all the socks. Everything was too big, men's boots, heavy socks, the pistol a swollen ankle tucked into the tops of my boots. They didn't touch it. I was safe. A Thing dressed in snow came in, shut the enormous door.

"The pigeons see what you're doing. Then crows rearrange everything," I explained.

"Shut up, Bird Woman," a stick figure in long shadows

in a bed next to me said loudly in an old woman's voice.

"They'll lift your skin away while you're sleeping," I warned the old woman.

"Now calm down in here," the white Thing said. "This is a hospital. We're only trying to make you all better." Her blue eyes penetrated me, and then moved away.

"I know what you're doing."

"Me too," the old woman said. "And it isn't pretty."

"Okay, ladies, calm down. I'm just trying to take your vitals. We won't do anything to you that you don't want us to do."

"You're a catalogue," I said. "I don't like you touching my feet."

"No one will touch your feet." She looked at my chart. "What's your name?"

"Jane."

"Last name?"

"Doe." Ray me.

She gave me an empty look, one that men back from war used. "We're fixing your stomach right now, Jane." She looked at my arms, "You took some IVs out."

She hovered. I received the jolt of something in my arms like flowers did at first daylight. I started to tug at the new tubes but she slapped my hands. "No, don't touch them."

"I'm flooded."

"Leave them be. That'll fix your stomach. Or else I'll have to get an orderly in here to stand watch over you all the time and you wouldn't like that. Or we could strap you down. And you wouldn't like that either."

I tried to spit at her but nothing was moving in my mouth. I lay my head back on the cool, fresh pillow. "Pieces of me are coming off."

"Do you want some kind of a bath?"

"I'm architecturally complete."

"I'll put that down as a 'maybe.'" She was writing things down, which meant that the words could swarm anywhere. "Now, I'd also like someone to come in soon and talk to you, Jane. Would that be okay?"

"Red is for counterfeiter's," I was just beginning to tell my new story to the little crow on top of the far mirror who had nowhere to land with all that white everywhere.

Jimmy, Chapter Fourteen

No matter what I did, Martine and Phillip's memories were fading. I stopped at the subway station but the motion of all that metal was sad, even if, for the passengers, it was precisely on time. I already lived in a city of memories and history. I looked for Natasha, her cart and the smell of fermentation. There was only a homeless man with a scraggly beard sitting on the bench I usually sat on. He held up a sign that said *If you haven't decided about me yet—then help* with an outstretched, crushed-looking hat at his feet.

I had searched for photographs of Martine and Phillip and found two, an overlit passport photo of Martine, where her nose was as thin and rigid as a pencil, and one with Martine leaning toward Phillip, who was under a tree holding a ball. Her hair was falling in folds around her neck. I had pinned the photos up over my bedroom mirror. My thoughts kept on returning to those two moments, one when Martine had to travel away from me and one when she tried to gather up Phillip and his ball. I felt left out. I was losing the other moments. I took the two photographs down and tucked them into a drawer so I could remember the other times. Lately I'd needed to examine the two photographs just to recall their faces. I wondered what Martine would have thought of Rosemary. *She good woman. Good woman for you if you get her.*

I sat. The homeless man slipped off his shoes, curled the laces around his torn soles, leaned his sign against the bench legs. He pocketed his change and left the crushed hat on the ground as he stood. He walked toward the tracks just as the wind and noise and what looked like moonlight approached through the long tunnel, highlighting everyone's expectant faces. People huddled closer to the tracks. I remembered Martine's wishful face turned up, toward my apartment. She was bringing me a present. She was holding Phillip's hand. They were crossing the street. She was dragging him. He was glancing at a new comic book. I waved at them from my window. Martine's features were nervous, happy, leafy. It was summer and very green and the whole world was ours and watching to see what we were going to do with it.

I had time to tremble and call out to them to watch out just as the fast car turned around the corner and sped down our street. The driver, a young man, didn't see them as they stepped in front of his car. Martine smiled and then fear embroidered her features. She glanced quickly at Phillip and pulled him closer to her. They held each other. Phillip closed his eyes and pushed his head against her stomach. The car left their bodies gnawed and bleeding in the street. The distraught driver stopped at the end of the block with his bloody car.

I never knew what she had meant to do. Had she done it on purpose? She couldn't get a divorce and she was going to be officially deported soon because her husband had alerted the authorities, saying it had been a fake marriage. She wouldn't tell me much about him for my own safety. There was nothing we could do except run and how far would we all get? I found out later, after the police rummaged through her body, that she was pregnant. She was cradling too much inside.

After the thud, people on the street circled their bodies but didn't touch them. Phillip and Martine were gone so suddenly and I couldn't stand to look at their bodies. One tiny dark mangled one and one larger one torn open and crushed. Blood trickled onto the road beneath them. I wanted to cry or do something but it was too late. I found myself frozen, outside among the horde of people. The police told me I lay down in the tiny space between their two bodies, shut my eyes, until they lifted me out. I wondered later why blood stains appeared on the sides of my clothes but not on the front. I didn't remember doing that.

What had Rosemary or THEM thought I could have done? Stopped the car? Stopped the government from deporting them? We were trapped by more than circumstances. Martine didn't leave me a note. The present she was bringing me was a drawing Phillip had done of me reading but it was dirty, torn, destroyed in the accident too.

The waiting people in the subway station, each believed they were alone and on their separate way toward their particular destination. They gasped as the homeless man jumped down onto the tracks. The bright light danced against his hair and one side of his face and emaciated body. He raised his dirty hands, looking lonely in the half light. His eyes grazed mine for a second. I ran to him, without thinking. I yanked him partially onto the platform. He was too heavy for me. A fat man grabbed him by the pants and pulled him the rest of the way up. People were too stunned to move. I heard voices beyond my panting. I lay on the cement platform. My heart flinched and stopped a moment before it began again, steadily. The train light came and went right through me, stopping slightly forward of us like something bright that had fallen out of the sky. The other two men were lying near me as though we had been intimate.

"Wow," someone said.

"Good job guys," someone else said, rushing by.

"Are you all okay?" another person asked.

I wanted to be forgiven.

All the people around us got onto the train. It was like a milk carton that had emptied and would be refilled again. The new people had no idea what had just happened. The fat man rose, nodded at me and then hurried up the stairs. "I'm late for work now," was all he said.

A policeman approached me and the homeless man, who was tall and dusting himself off. I sat on the bench. I wanted to tell the policeman that nothing fit me.

"Why?" I asked the homeless man but he just made a strange gesture at me and wiped his mouth.

"What's going on here?" the policeman inquired.

The homeless man began pointing at me. "This man's been fucking with my life."

***

Emily took my hand and coaxed me onto one of the subways that led toward the beach. Aaron was with caregivers and I searched for the homeless man I'd help save, but I hadn't seen him at the station since that incident. Maybe he finished what he had started. I didn't know.

"I haven't really gone anywhere on the trains since visiting Rosemary. And before that I hadn't gone anywhere in a long time."

"According to my old notes you just like to watch trains go by." She was wearing flat shoes, some kind of short pants, a blousy shirt, a jacket around her waist, and a large, round red hat that hit something every time she turned her head. "Or maybe it's the people you're watching."

"Both probably." She released my hand.

"It'll do you some good to actually go somewhere you haven't been before. It'll make you look at things differently." We were sitting in all that hurtling metal. Everyone looked too real.

"You're getting awfully wise, Emily." We were sitting side by side, jostled back and forth. Her hat alternately hit the side of my head and the dark window scratched with names in back of us. I could feel extra flesh shaking at my stomach. "What did you learn on your trip to the sea?"

"That I'm not easily contented. And that I need to pick my battles."

I nodded. She was wise.

"It surprises me what goes in and out of our heads. I just hope I hold onto the important stuff," she said. She picked up my sore fingers and tugged, so we both stood. Young and old, both faded under the lights. "We need to change twice more." We danced on the floor until the train stopped.

"I saved a homeless man's life the other day, but it didn't really mean anything."

"To who?"

"He wasn't happy about it." Her hat bumped me near my eye as we ran hand in hand and jumped onto another train that opened. At the fading station I saw two people from THEM with pamphlets standing near the turnstiles apprehensively.

"I hate to ask, but how are things going with Rosemary?"

This train resembled the last one only with different ads above our heads. I liked the sensation of being squeezed into new geography. "I don't know. I'm waiting to see what will happen. What she'll decide." I didn't want to burden her with my adult problems although Emily was probably used to that. "I wonder how things will go."

"Are you getting some sleep?"

"Not much."

"Of course I think it's all her fault. That's a bad position to be in for you, just waiting. But I know it well." She nodded her head and her hat grazed my ear.

"Where did you get that hat?" I brushed the edge away.

"A thrift store. Do you like it? I bet it belonged to someone glamorous, someone from your time."

"How old do you think I am?"

"Old."

This time she grabbed my sleeve as we caught our last

subway train. The last station was painted with more cheerful colors and was filled with more natural light. People's clothes were unraveling, casual. They seemed to be practicing the art of loitering. It was a different world. I imagined a city where everyone wore big hats but I wondered how many people escaped with undamaged eyes. I was short of breath.

The last subway's route was partially above the ground and I was watching the curves of streets and roads, buildings and windows that were rectangular in the usual way, for a moment, and then they were gone. Like life. I watched clouds converge onto one another and separate into newly formed shapes. They were daydreaming about unknown cities too.

When we emerged and made our way past some dilapidated buildings scrawled with words that made no sense, we came to a beach crawling with people and dizzy with light. The smell of fried food was everywhere and barefoot children ran all over. Sand sprayed from their churning feet. There were dripping ice cream cones, hot dogs, and brightly colored beach umbrellas and towels. The odor of sweat and salt permeated everything. I could see waves studded with people, but I couldn't hear them past all the noise.

"Come," Emily said, "I found a place a bit farther away from this crowd." She started to take my hand but thought better of it in front of all these people. The people might have wondered who was leading who.

"It *is* a bit noisy here."

She led me to a place where we sat on chunks of old

cement, but we could hear the whisper of waves above the din of commingled voices. People didn't seem to venture too much further than the half circle of warm sand and pebbles and food shacks. Some tall grass had grown up between the crumbled cement and stirred. Between us and the horizon lay sand, vast splashing water, sky. It was pleasant to reach my arm out and not touch a wall or person. A landscape larger than I could imagine stretched out in front of us. Everything in the city was small and contained. I was always bumping into something. Here there was air. I thought about a city under the ocean, everyone floating around. I sat, arranging myself so that nothing would bend and cause me pain.

Emily lay down on her jacket. "I still haven't decided what to do about my virginity."

"I don't think I want to hear this, Emily."

"Oh come on, you old fart. I'm just thinking out loud. It isn't like I'd ask you to do anything about it." She turned onto her side and fixed her blue eyes on me.

"Well, if I was you, I'd wait for the right time and the right person."

"That's all you do is wait." She lay on her back, looking at the sky. "This virginity is annoying. My mother and friends think it's something to get over."

I sighed. "I'm not surprised."

"I thought Hammer was the one..." She turned on her side again. "What about you? What was your first time like?"

"Oh Emily. I'm a man and an old one. It's different for me."

"Come on, answer the question." She unearthed some sunglasses and balanced them on her nose. "Come on, confess."

"It was a very long time ago, during the war, in a foreign country." You always remembered it even if you wanted to forget.

"Was it paid or unpaid?"

"Sort of paid." I forgot to buy sunglasses. I shielded my eyes with one hand.

"Did you have anyone back home?"

"Sort of. But that didn't work out. When I came home she was married."

"Bummer." She sounded like she meant it. She was picking sand out of her fingernails.

"I've had a long full life."

Emily looked up. "Is it over?"

I shook my head.

"No kids? That you know of anyway."

"No. Your life'll probably be different than you imagined."

"Probably. Because I want to grow up and become a Mormon, marry, and have tons of kids." She laughed. Her red hat giggled. "Just kidding. What will you do with Aaron when he's eighteen, in a few years?"

"I don't know. I haven't really thought that far ahead. Besides, I don't know what to do with him now."

"You need to talk to him. He knows a lot. He told me that I have too much personality. I told him that he had too little. He wrote 'I'm a story that doesn't show any time passing.' Your sessions with him have certainly improved his writing."

I dug my fist into my chin and rested my elbows against my cramped knees. I peered over the water into a pale nothingness. It was relaxing. "His group doesn't seem to care about him much anymore. I suppose I could do almost anything I want with him."

"Can I do what I want with him too?"

"Like what?" I added, "I'm trying to avoid trouble."

"Old man, I think you need more trouble." Emily threw her red hat at me but I ducked and she missed me.

***

Rosemary whispered into the telephone, "I'll come over and we'll see if you can figure out what to do with me."

It was evening. I watched someone across the street's lit window in this blue-toned city. The woman was walking toward a little boy. She was wearing glasses and a sea-green dress. The boy was dressed as a sailor. The woman glanced at me as if she knew me. Maybe she did. Then she closed her curtains. Lights sprung up everywhere and stayed in place while people and their pets traveled all around them.

"The boy's asleep."

"I'm not coming to see the boy."

"What about Brian?"

"We're officially disengaged right now." Her voice was sleepy like syrup.

"Are you sure?"

"Are you trying to talk me out of you?" She laughed lightly. "Brian is easy not to marry."

"You're a difficult woman."

"And you're a difficult, old man."

I made coffee, left the kitchen light on so I could see the edges of the defunct television. I sat on the sofa. Rosemary's laughter had been so light and musical, not at all like her speaking voice. I remembered her rare laugh again and again, replaying it. I wanted to hold onto her braids, climb them like rope. I could bury myself in her. Her bland features were beginning to wrinkle, her skin looked soft and powdery. She had a jagged gray hairline and thick ankles. How would she describe me? Thin, old, cranky, too intellectual, not enough emotional life. I didn't know how to fight for someone I cared about. I was out of practice. There was so much to learn. We would have time. Martine had been twenty years ago. I smiled into the darkness, my lips imitating a sliver of moon. My coffee was bitter and good. The building grew quiet. Apartment lights flickered on. I watched the darkness change. It was hard to tell what was what in the dark living room.

I waited. I unlocked the door. At least Rosemary knew all about the boy. I imagined day trips, ferries, wandering in some woods, rocky cliffs, unfamiliar hotels, scabby roads other people wouldn't travel on, forgetting the time, losing our sense of place, finishing whatever our bodies had begun and liking it. I wanted to pat her into shape like clay. I looked at the clock and couldn't believe the time. Several hours had passed. I called Rosemary's phone number and let it ring. Nothing. I stood and placed my cold cup into the sink. At the window I couldn't see any movement, not even cats or taxicabs or buses. I heard the rumble of early garbage trucks dividing the streets in their noisy work. Then newspaper delivery began with thuds as some of the coffee shops and magazine stands grew slowly radiant with light. It was still night outside, yet the city sounds were creeping in, a few stray cars came by. I peeked in on the boy, but he was still sleeping. There was a prickling in my legs and the muscles around my spine were tender from nothing.

I waited until that thin piece of the moon disappeared and people outside were beginning to go to work. I called Rosemary's number again. Then I called THEM.

"I'm looking for Rosemary, the woman with gray braids who usually wears plaid clothes." I gave the woman (it sounded like the same woman I had talked to before) Rosemary's last name and address and phone number.

"Hold on."

She put me on hold indefinitely.

"We don't have anybody by that name here."

I was alarmed. I gave her the address and phone number she had previously given me.

"That location is owned by THEM. But I don't know that phone number or name."

"The woman that was going to marry Brian. The older woman with gray braids."

"Our Brian is already married," she answered.

"How many times can he get married?" I was being facetious.

"You're right. He can marry more than one woman since he's Brian."

"That doesn't seem fair." I couldn't.

"Anyway I don't know who you're describing."

"Brian introduced her at a meeting the other night."

"I wasn't there. I'm sorry. I don't know who you mean."

"She can't have suddenly disappeared." I was nearly screaming. "She was coming to see me last night."

"You know we don't use our real names here at THEM anyway." She hung up the phone.

I called back twice. She hung up on me.

I woke up the boy. He was wan and tired when I turned on the lights. I could see his shoulder bones and arms muscling as he sat up in bed. He was blinking. *No, no, no.* Or he was just blinking from being disturbed.

"What do you know about Rosemary being gone?" I was trying to control my voice. I threw paper and a pen onto the bed and they bounced along his hidden torso.

Rosemary has a big heart. But I have cultivated indifference. Is that so surprising?

I blinked *no* but the boy couldn't see me. Sarcasm wouldn't help anyway. "Do you have any idea where she is?"

She could be anywhere but here.

I was sorry for a moment that he had learned to write so well. "You don't know anything more about her disappearance?"

It's worrisome. The time is wrong. The world doesn't fit well and I am the one left here.

"So she didn't talk to you?"

He blinked *no. The staircase seems to be a good place to cry.*

"I didn't know she was so unhappy. I knew about her mother."

Wishes can be faulty like the body.

"Brian is wrong about you. You'd make a wonderful leader, Aaron."

He blinked *yes* and said *thank you* with his hands.

I wasn't exactly being complimentary. "People have been shot and I'm worried about her."

The boy's eyes opened wide although he couldn't see anything. He wrote *Everyone is just passing through.*

"Where?" But I knew he couldn't answer since he didn't know anything about the world.

***

I took the subways I had taken previously to Rosemary's apartment. I left the boy alone. He would be fine. I looked for Natasha in the depths of the station nearest me, but I couldn't find her anywhere. I searched under the wide concrete stairs, in corners, on the farthest benches. I peeked over a poorly dressed woman's newspaper, that she was in the process of reading, but it wasn't Natasha. I needed to go, to find Rosemary. The subway journey was noncommittal, the usual opening and closing doors, the usual people. This time the gothic building loomed from several streets away with its severe, misshaped rooftop creatures whose impending flight looked imminent. Strange animals were carved into the edifice. The windows reflected a flotilla of birds on its glass, soon the birds disappeared. My hopes rose toward that sky as if it was a benevolent and knowing heaven. Then they dropped as I pushed open the dusty, thick door. I wanted to be rational, explain the situation. A tall man with dark, slicked hair stood whispering over a black telephone. His eyes darted everywhere in the large, ornate room. My feet sank into the luxurious carpet and approached the man as if they had a desire of their own. An enormous metal chandelier perched over our heads. I was in a story that wasn't my own. I didn't have a will.

"Is Rosemary here?" I tapped on the counter, so he knew I meant it.

The man looked stunned. "Rosemary?" He brought out a book. "There's no Rosemary here. Sometimes the owners rent out their apartments but..." he perused the book, "there's no Rosemary listed as renting or owning here."

My fist hit the wooden counter and the book flew upward and then settled down again. I gave him her last name. "I saw her here not very long ago."

The man looked frightened now. "I'm sorry, sir, but there's no such person here."

I described her. I had Emily and the boy as proof. "I met her here with several other people."

"I'm sorry, sir, I don't know of anyone with that name."

"She lives here with her mother that died recently in the fifth floor apartment on the left."

He seemed perplexed. He measured the light against my face. There was a silence like there was often with the boy.

The lobby was quiet and appeared to go on forever with its colors that couldn't be found anywhere anymore. The world changed incrementally. We watched its comings and goings. I wanted to hold onto something.

"I'm lost and stubborn," I told him.

"Come with me." He removed a key from a pigeonhole behind him.

We entered the arthritic elevator and it haltingly took us to the fifth floor. "Is this the apartment?" he asked.

I nodded and he opened the door. Our breathing echoed into a large, empty apartment. There wasn't any furniture. No black cloth or mirrors. I shuffled from room to vacant room. The walls were an old, forsaken, beige color with dark streaks. I found a bent silver spoon on the floor, kicked to the side, but nothing else. The spoon wasn't proof of anything. There was the smell of molding carpet and sugar but no food, no human activities. The man watched me, then ran his hands through his greasy hair.

"You looked like you needed to see this."

"Who owns it?" I was looking down at squirrels digging in the grass outside. The sun lined the window frame.

"It's really none of my business."

***

Harold fixed his soft, brown eyes on mine. Then he looked elsewhere. He was the only person I recognized at the meeting. His beard was shaped into a perfect triangle and he wore a scarf and the usual neat clothes, black tee shirt, white pants. I wanted to scream at everyone, wring their necks until they told me where Rosemary was. Was she still alive? Did she care for me at all? Was her name even Rosemary? There was a part of me that wanted to run away, be done with everyone, including the boy. What did I deserve? I was a silly, old man who might have lost his one chance for love. I knew there were other bigger catastrophes than mine.

I sauntered over to Harold, past the folding chairs in the large, dusty room. The windows were so dirty all the cars looked like lumbering animals catching up to some herd somewhere. I shook his hand. He held his coffee in his other hand. He was the only black man in the room. "Hi, Harold. My name's Jimmy. I remember you from the last meeting."

"Yeah, you're the one who asks all those questions."

"That's me," I said cheerfully. He didn't look thrilled.

"Well you're here again, so are you joining? Or have you already joined?"

"Hey, man, I have a question for you." I grabbed a hot coffee, stirred the muddy waters of my cup.

He nodded.

"Do you remember that woman at the last meeting who they announced was going to marry Brian?"

"Hmm," he pulled at his beard, made an inviolable face. "Maybe. I'm not sure. I thought Brian was already married."

"Don't you remember Rosemary with the gray braids?" I peered at him intently. "Didn't you speak to her?"

"Hey, look, are you accusing me of something?" His hands flew into the air and he backed away from me.

"No, of course not." I moved away from him. "Don't you remember her? I'm just trying to find her."

He was looking at someone else across the expanse of the room whose finger cut across his throat. Someone I didn't recognize. "Hmm," he said, "I can't say that I do remember her. Gray braids, huh? Nope, I don't remember nobody like that."

"Oh, c'mon," I punched his arm, spilling both coffees. "You've got to remember her. She's so argumentative it's hard to forget her."

"Hey, man, look around the room." His arm spread wide. He grinned. He focused on a young woman with red hair talking animatedly to a sad-looking man with glasses and unbolted wrinkles on his forehead. We heard something about "humdrum receipts and lots of wrong answers..." They wore matching black and white outfits. "There are lots of women here, some good-looking too."

"I want Rosemary." I said pointedly.

He patted me on the shoulder. "Good luck with that. I don't remember her. But you can ask other people." Harold's eyes darted around the room and alighted in the kitchen area. He straightened his scarf, walked toward a brisk blonde who was closing a cupboard.

I sat. I felt helpless. I waited.

Brian arrived. He was disguised as an old man, but I didn't take it personally. At least he was an old man with a long, white beard and mustache. He wore thick glasses and his meaty hands appeared too young. He wore a wedding ring. He had an old fashioned hat with a brim, which he removed along with his other implements for hiding. Then he rose to the podium and delivered a speech titled "Devotion in the Worst Way." Afterwards I pushed by some people and arrived at Brian and the men assigned to keep him safe.

"Where's Rosemary?"

"You know we don't use our real names here." He smiled benignly at me. "Besides, after forsaking the privilege of being my next wife, she disappeared. I don't know where she is but if you do find her, let us know. We still have some things to discuss." He donned his disguise and left.

I was losing myself while searching for Rosemary. I didn't need a disguise. I was angry but then I grew worried. Pieces of me were frantic. I'd lost someone before. I was losing memories about Rosemary at an accelerated pace, compared to Martine.

I watched Harold weaving among the women at the meeting. I wished Brian or someone like him could turn water into wine, a table into a chair, the dead into the living. Were we what we believed we were? Is that what belief could do? I wanted back my years of undoing. I'd made too many mistakes.

CARLY, CHAPTER FIFTEEN

I woke up screaming in all that white. It sounded like it was coming from me. I stopped. I heard a cart creaking at the door, the tiny wheels turning and clicking, the way it usually moaned for me, with all that metal and understanding. I smelled food. A Dead Thing dressed in white was pushing it. I wanted to put my arms around it. It was covered in clean linen and had breakfast trays stacked between layers of metal. I looked at it more carefully. It had changed. I yelled some more anyway.

"Where are my clothes?" I was ashamed. My hand shot to my socks, the ghost-maker, my boots. They were all there, untouched and waiting.

"Right there, Bird Woman," the old woman voice said. "Right where the nurse left them. We're all pretty naked here."

I grabbed my folded clothes and started to put them on over the long, thin, blue flag with the flap in the back. The blue was dissolving my body. One of the crows pointed out that my stomach wasn't hurting anymore.

"They won't let you go yet so you might as well calm down, eat some food, have a discussion with one of your birds." The voice sat up in bed, shifted its blanket. A veil surrounded the bed.

I couldn't see it. "Who the fuck are you?" I pushed my clothes aside and lay in the bed.

"Are you talking to me?"

I looked around, a silhouette danced on the other side of its curtain. "Who the fuck do you think I'm talking to?"

"I can't always tell, maybe one of your birds. My name's Susan. What's yours really?"

"Natasha. All this blue is hurting me."

"I'm sick and tired of all this crappy food and being woken up in the middle of the night. I've been here three days." Large bumps moved behind her curtain.

"What did the Dead Things do to you?" I snatched my breakfast tray from a woman with a jangling mouth. I gulped the food down from all the tiny compartments.

"You seem to know them well enough. Right you are, they're all dead inside," the empty, mewling woman said. "I can't tell you how I ended up in here. I was hit on the head and left for dead. Someone was trying to kill me."

I felt full and my stomach was good. The crow circled, pecking at me to relax, to sleep, after eating that concoction of good food. The Things' cart left, leaking breakfasts. When I turned around, the crow was missing. "My body is good inside. But my brain is too hairy."

She said, "Being here makes me question everything too."

"I need to find the Dis, that boy, and the old man. That's what the crow said."

"Well, if that's what the crow said then it has to be true." She shifted. "The nurse told me they're sending in the psychiatrist to talk to you."

"That birdhouse tells us what we've done then clouds

fall through my fingers like diseases. Air trickles in here and shows me the way out."

"I don't mind it here, three square meals a day and a bed to sleep on. And nobody can find me here since I don't use my real name anymore. It isn't bad."

"That Brian is full of bad news and tricks that make you into somebody else, to make you famous."

"Oh, are you with THEM too? You know, because Brian is my son, they've been making me wear disguises. We always change our names anyway. But especially now that people are getting hurt and nobody seems to know why." She laughed in an old-fashioned way. "It helped me a lot as you can see."

"Just ignore yourself and you'll become another, bit by bit."

"Thanks for the advice." The tiresome woman stirred in her bed.

"With clues I can find my way through the city. I'll just follow the color of their eyes." I leaped into my clothes, threw the blue flag I'd been wearing on the too-shiny floor. "I'll fill myself up like a breeze since I know what they're doing."

I touched her curtain with my elbow by mistake. But what I saw terrified me. Behind the hospital curtain large black wings unfolded and spread out around the old woman on the bed. She flapped once or twice. I held my mouth shut, stopped it from saying, "I know what you're doing" because I didn't know her nonhuman ways.

As I bounded out the door I heard the old woman's voice say to me, "See you in another life."

Jimmy, Chapter Sixteen

"I've lost Rosemary," I told Aaron. "I can't seem to find her anywhere and I've run out of places to look for her."

Stop looking then.

"Yes, maybe I'll find her when I'm not looking. I remember calling what was left of Martine's family in the islands and telling them about Martine and Phillip's accident. They wailed across the phone lines, especially about Phillip. He was so young and sweet. 'They no come home again,' her mother said. It took me a long time to cry. The apartment was so empty. I didn't want to come home. I sent her family their possessions, except for the photographs. I couldn't bear to look at what they owned. I guess I've grown into myself too much. I'm not exactly a barrel of laughs." I was brushing his hair, then his teeth.

He blinked noncommittally, random yeses and nos. Maybe he was just blinking.

"At my age it's a lot to do anything. Everything hurts and nothing works the way it should."

The boy picked up his pen and paper. *Don't want to be a burden.*

"I'll go up and invite Emily to come down here for a while. You'd like that, wouldn't you, Aaron?"

One blink, one blink, one blink.

"Rosemary couldn't have just disappeared into thin air."

Although I knew that people only saw what they wanted to see. How many times early on had I walked into the boy's room expecting him to be a whole person? Not blind, mute, or lame. I'd had to adjust to the truth each time.

Try a road devoid of anything polite.

"I've tried the police, hospitals, accident reports but I don't know what name she'd be using."

Sometimes in the company of others we want to be somewhere else.

"And your point is?"

Maybe she hasn't really disappeared.

"Has she changed right under my nose?"

When there are several paths opening up people have more choices and they usually pick one they can touch.

I needed someone to interpret. I needed someone who was impartial. I couldn't weep for Rosemary or be angry with her or kiss her hello or goodbye. I was left suspended, waiting. Maybe I already misunderstood the clues. I was a tiny person living in a tiny apartment. The boy lived in his body but I wasn't sure whether he was a tiny person or not. I didn't think so.

Maybe your greatest moment is coming.

"Isn't that always true? Isn't that what we're always hoping for?"

One blink, *yes.*

"I always feel as if you know something I don't."

Two blinks, *no.*

"So you don't think Brian did anything to Rosemary or whatever her name is?"

He has cars full of women. She's a golden ticket.

"It's hard to know what's going on."

How many false prophets are there?

"It's so difficult."

You know the secret language of the lost. You can find her.

I didn't find his answers reassuring but then neither did I find them disheartening. It was a start. Maybe Emily could help.

I ran upstairs, called "Emily" at her front door. Luckily, Emily, with wet hair, opened the door. Her mother was playing some music and dancing with a large man, who looked deficient. Emily looked small and thin and childlike. I could have picked her up and carried her like a suitcase. I was tempted.

"I'll come down in a minute, as soon as I dry my hair."

I nodded. My thoughts became too many random thoughts. I sat on the stairs between the apartments. It was still quiet. Traffic hurled itself forward and backwards outside, and the occasional sound of a television nearby punctured my thinking. It was a small apartment building with three or four apartments on each floor and people with small lives that fit into city-sized rooms. I thought of a city full of mazes and how nothing would ever get accomplished or found. The stairway was dark and winding and dusty, footprints everywhere.

I was accustomed to the boy, strange as he was. He had become a part of me, one that I didn't always understand.

I was accustomed to relating to people's ideas of themselves that were replacing the real people. The idea of a woman couldn't make dinner or kiss. I was quickly becoming a keeper of memories.

Did I want too much? There was no harm in hoping and the heart certainly had its own direction. I didn't expect much, especially at my age. I had nothing much to lose. There was a freedom in that.

I bounded downstairs. My eyes were leaking when Emily came down, her damp hair clinging to her shoulders. I wanted to wring her out. I told her so and she laughed.

"Are you my mother?"

"Do I look like her?"

We sat for a moment in my living room. I surveyed my life, a few pieces of fraying furniture in my vast apartment and Aaron. And there I was in charge of all that loneliness. No wonder my wild white hair fell out.

"Aaron's been asking for you. Are you okay with seeing him?" He could hear us. Our eyes met. I thought of a pigeon trying to eat seed but ending up throwing most of it around.

"I've even brought my own pad and pen." She held her usual notebook aloft like a prize.

I opened Aaron's door and let Emily in. The boy's soapy eyes shifted toward us. He squinted as though he could almost see us. His hands gestured in his own sign language. He wanted Emily to sit. He smiled weakly. I left the door open as I backed out of the room. I didn't trust the boy, or Emily. I picked up a book in the living room, leaving them to their semi-privacy. I didn't know what the boy wrote or what he wanted. I could only hear Emily's part of the conversation.

"What do you think?" "I didn't think of that." "I'm not really in school anymore. So it doesn't matter." "Yeah, like two ugly, prickly beasts trying to go at each other. Yuck." Her sweet, high voice. "I see what you mean, how two philosophies can't be joined. What can we do?" "No, and what do you mean by 'unknowing,' 'sentimental,' and 'a group'?" "I don't always understand what you're trying to say. But there's a part of me that believes I might know. Maybe like the way we understand dreams. Or think we do."

A longer pause.

"Yeah, I guess people sometimes do change. And that stuff sounds good, but no, no kissing."

I went to Aaron's door, knocked. "Okay," I said, "visiting hours are over."

"Let's check out that acrobatic place. I think Aaron is willing, if not able," Emily said.

"Maybe you and I should go first and see what it's like before we bring Aaron," I said.

***

In the subway station a young woman I didn't recognize from THEM, in the usual black and white, stood huddled with a group of people in the smoking area. Her blonde hair bloomed on one side of her face but not the other. She said to someone, "Yeah, they say that self-denial makes you stronger." She inhaled deeply then allowed coils of smoke to escape her mouth slowly and circle toward the cement ceiling. "But what can you do when you can't help your-self?"

She was a different kind of believer than I'd heard before. Maybe they were moving closer to my side, the more fallible side. I was beginning to see their point. Every encounter had so much more meaning than I had believed was possible. I found myself wanting to go over to the young woman and argue.

I relaxed there, in the agitation of the trains. Their metal had an appetite, snatching people from each side, spitting them out. That appetite was contagious. People ran to catch a train that mumbled away. A dank liquid oozed from one of the walls. I sat on a bench. Natasha crept from behind a wall.

"You look worse for wear," I said. She had never looked well, under all those rags, but it was hard to tell. Her eyes were smoldering, her knit cap askew, her hair shorn. She was muttering instructions to the noisy walls, her hands skittering.

"It's these god damn crows. Pestering me about things." One gloved hand twisted in the air. She whirled around toward me. "I took a little vacation," she blurted out. "It did me good. I know the way of things now. I know what everyone is doing." She rubbed her stomach.

"You have to explain things to me sometime. Have you seen an older woman with gray braids? I think her name's Rosemary. I've been looking for her."

She sniffed. "There's murder in the wind and what's not said is important."

I continued, "She might use a different name. She's with THEM."

She perked up at the group's name. "That Brian hurts me all the time." She held her red knit head in her gloved hands. "And those Things," she yelled, pointing at people. Her hand at her mouth confidentially, "Some are dead, you know."

She sat. She looked deflated on my bench. I could smell her bad odor across the distance between us. Her cart was off to the side. There was something Shakespearean about her. Maybe there was too much tragedy and comedy between the two of us. "I think I told you I worked around trains all my life, different kinds of trains. I find it relaxing here."

"I've had dreams." Her clothes snarled around her as she shifted.

I sighed. "Most of them don't work out well." The disorder of her mind often seemed orderly. She reminded me of the boy.

She patted her obedient cart. "We're little specks of things made up of little specks of things moving all over." She patted a small lump in her sock. "The bigger cuts don't hurt as much." She began searching for something in her cart. She pulled out a brightly colored child's necklace with big, round beads, and put it around my neck. "Here's protection for your quest."

"Thank you, Natasha." It was plastic, lightweight, and silly. It smelled like rotten food.

"My name's Patty."

"I thought it was Natasha."

"Depends on the day." She was looking for something. "Here." She held out a toy telescope.

I took it.

She unfurled a palm gloved in a dirty piece of leather. I put five dollars in it and her hand curled around the money, withdrawing it into her coat. She cackled and seemed pleased. I held up the toy telescope as a train and then another one came into the station. I adjusted my stance so I could see into the windows. All the people were posed for that moment in the insistent light. On the next train a woman, with long, gray braids down the back of a pink jacket, sat with her back towards me under the flooding, sharp light. I focused the play telescope on her. It couldn't be Rosemary.

I walked to another angle and saw Rosemary's face, but it had make-up and red lipstick. It was wearing a gold necklace I'd never seen. She seemed unfamiliar. The woman moved her braids to the top of her head and pinned them into a bun. I realized it was her, but that she looked different.

I screamed, "Rosemary." The woman lurched forward, obviously startled, but she didn't turn.

"Rosemary." I was sure.

I ran but the train had closed its doors and was hurtling into the tunnel, groaning. My hair and clothes flapped in its wake, in my forward motion. I stopped running after it. My body was full of grievances. I was panting, sweating, and still clutching the flimsy telescope in my fist. Was I wicked or righteous? Maybe I was in between. Maybe I didn't deserve her. I sat on a bench. I wanted to lay exhausted on the ground, but I kept on thinking how Rosemary was still alive.

***

The guys at the diner were watching a television affixed to a shelf in the corner. They looked mesmerized. The television light, which resembled apparitions, was flickering on their upturned faces. Sunlight streamed through the diner windows onto the mustard-colored tables. All that stainless steel inside gleamed. The waitress stood still, her eyes on the screen, a plate of food and a drink in her hands.

Jack twisted his head toward me. "That's a fine mess you've gotten yourself into, Jimmy, with that religious group. They're killing each other off like in gang wars." He spit into his glass.

"Who told you about THEM?" But I knew as soon as I asked who it was. "Doesn't Emily have anything better to do?"

"Unfortunately not," Bill said, "I've been encouraging her to go back to school or at least get a G.E.D."

"What do you think you can keep from us and why would you bother? You know we're your friends, right?" Don said, adjusting his glasses.

"What did Emily tell you?"

"About your cockamamie group?" Jack put his napkin over his mouth. "Oops, I didn't mean it like that." He looked at me, "Although they are getting picked off like flies."

"Yeah," the waitress was repositioning her food plates, "what're you thinking? What about all those regular religions?"

"Why didn't you tell us?" Bill asked.

"I don't know. It's complicated and I don't need shit from you guys, which I'm getting now anyway. So did Emily say anything else?"

"No, good God, Jimmy, is there more? This is enough of a surprise."

"Now's the time to confess it all, my son." Don was imitating a priest, holding a napkin high at his plaid shirt collar.

"Has Emily been here often without me?"

All three of them looked at one another. "Not that much," Don said. "She just needs a little guidance."

"Us old guys are going to help a teenage girl?"

"Don't forget me." The waitress was moving among her other customers, delivering white plates filled with food. She lifted a finger.

"Yeah, why not?" Jack drank something, pointed at the television where Brian's face, then an older woman's, flashed on the screen.

The older woman was speaking to reporters in a thin, wavering voice. She appeared distressed. I noticed Harold, the younger blonde woman from the train station who had questions, the man with the ponytail who seemed to be everywhere, all standing behind the older woman. A reporter encapsulated, "This is Brian's mother and she had an attempt on her life. She hasn't seen Brian in some time now and is worried about his whereabouts. If anyone knows anything she's hoping they'll step forward, especially with all the recent deaths among the groups' members. His mother now fears the worst has happened to him."

Were we all in danger? Was that why Rosemary left? Was she trying to disguise herself or was I seeing the real Rosemary and everything else had been a lie?

"Maybe we should hide you," Bill said.

"Yeah," Jack said, "some gun-toting nuts might come after you too. You're always welcome in my apartment, messy as it is. You know that, buddy." He hit me on my shoulder.

They were joking, but I had to ask. "Is there any pattern or reason for all this? Has the news said anything about why?"

"Naw, they think it's a power struggle between two religious factions. Who would ever think that people could kill for religion?" Jack was picking his teeth. "Maybe it's some shit within the group, something about the leadership."

"That could be." Aaron wasn't that important any more. We were probably safe.

"Don't you have any idea since you're a part of the group?" Don asked.

"I don't know. I have something that was once important to them."

"What?" Jack inquired.

"Nothing that's important now."

Jack's face twisted as though I'd punched him but there was no reason to tell them. I was embarrassed too.

"That's good. Otherwise we'd have to worry about you too," Don stated. "Maybe you should hide it."

"We're your oldest friends. You can tell us anything."

"God help you." We were back to the usual give and take.

"Yeah." The waitress was foodless and put her fists on her hips. "It seems like you sure have a lot to tell us, Jimmy." She laughed. "So how's our little Emily doing? Tell her we miss her here. Tell that sweet little child that she can come here anytime."

Jack guffawed. "Sweet little child. That kid could manipulate her way out of Sing Sing."

"Yeah," Bill said, "but we like having her here."

"So, Jimmy, what are you going to do about all this?" The waitress was too curious.

"Yeah, Jimmy, what do you make of all this?" Don asked.

"It should all be over soon."

"Wishful thinking," someone said.

***

I took subways all afternoon, into the evening. It was nice to keep on moving and not think too much about where I was going. I went to Emily's beach. I shuffled to the same cement formation we had visited. Long grass tickled my feet. Sand enveloped me as though I would become a part of it. I was shrinking. The sound of the waves was soothing. I watched two little girls poking at something near the water with a stick. Finally they flung it, whatever it was, wet and squishy, in the air and it landed with a thud. I didn't want to talk to anyone.

As a boy I used to hide in a cave near some cliffs when my parents fought or had friends over I didn't like. Maybe Rosemary wanted to disappear too.

I would wait for Rosemary where she could find me. She had to know that I was looking for her. Words could only do so much. Words were all some of us had.

I paced the damp part of the shore, kicking seaweed, stones, some broken shells, bottle caps, plastic food containers, driftwood. I peered at the top of the ocean, which was a whole unknown city in itself. There was so much turmoil below the surface, a meeting of memories. Each sea creature had its own perspective on events. Fish kept to their schools, following. Jellyfish were nebulous, whole worlds within themselves. Horseshoe crabs were prehistoric, frightening to look at, and I wondered what went on in their primitive brains. There were the dainty minnows, always off in different directions. Some microscopic life I could hardly see, but that mattered greatly in the pyramid of life.

What should I do or not do?

What or who should I pursue?

I ate two hot dogs at a shack owned by a guy covered in tattoos. He had a wide-legged walk and brutally strong hands. I strolled. It was getting crowded so I hopped onto the first train. The train zoomed above ground. I felt as though I was flying. The train passed a pigeon in midair.

The sign, where I got off, said 127th Street but I didn't know which borough. Asians, with beautiful black hair, clustered in shops. I was visiting someone else's life. I remembered where the subway entrance was so I could get back there. I could let my mind drift.

I saw some chickens hanging upside down in a red store-front with Chinese letters. I passed open markets with food in rows in the stalls and colorful clothes swinging from lines that hit me in the face as I walked past. There were bins full of shoes and knick-knacks that seemed to have no purpose. I was arranging my dislikes. The streets were crowded. I tried not to bump into passersby.

At the next stop telephone wires and airplanes cut the sky into geometric shapes. I smelled a yeasty bakery. It was a quieter residential street, lined with houses connected on each side, till the next street. Everything was laid out sym-metrically, alleyways, cars, even trash bins. A young man in overalls walked by me and nodded.

"Hi Frank," the man said.

Before I had time to correct him, he had passed by me.

"Hi," was all I said to his diminishing back. A woman in a nearby home was cleaning the windows. She opened and closed them, circling their glass with a wet rag.

She stood up from what she was doing and waved at me. "Hey, Frank," she yelled.

I waved back at her. It was beginning to rain. I could have stayed there. Used a disguise, become Frank. People needed to place a person. It was about context. There I could have had a different life.

CARLY, CHAPTER SEVENTEEN

I was wet below my knees. I was melting. I couldn't move without pushing the heaviest water aside. I scratched at walls, my fingernails poking out from my gloves. Garbage was rising. Tin cans cackled near my thighs, plastic prodded me, cigarette butts tapped my knees like instruments at the hospital. My clothes clung, crawled up my legs.

"Am I fighting for my life?" I asked my friend. I tried to swirl around in the water but I didn't go anywhere. I would have to learn how to swim.

"Fuck," he said, "this screws up my equilibrium." He slapped his ear with his hand. "Now I can't find my sleeping bag or any of my shit."

"That's too much looping around anyway." The water wanted to push us.

"Oh, man, I'm sorry. This is fucked. There were a bunch of us living here in the sewer, and now everything's gone." He began hitting his head with his hand.

I grabbed the ghost-maker from my sock, crouching. I put it inside my shirt. The sewer water was hugging me in a way I didn't like. Empty bottles bobbed just like on a carousel. Something striped and sinking was going by.

"There's a blanket." I handed the soggy mess to him. A tent was caught inside. "I like surprises." Like the old man. Like candy with something creamy inside.

I screamed at my cart up the stairs, near the entrance, "Don't come in here. It's a big, juicy mouth."

I was glad that my friend had made me leave my cart outside. We were detecting first. I hid my valuables but I was still afraid for my cart. My friend and I tried to hold onto the scabby walls. Other stuff took their place, soggy books or frames without pictures.

"Oh boy." My friend was wet to his waist and had stopped hitting himself. "We need to get out of here. The sewer'll spill into the subway soon. I guess it's all the rain. I don't know. Fuck," he said. "Maybe something's went bust. All my stuff's gone. Where the hell will we go?"

A ratdog with a strange smile on its face swam by. I wanted to catch it but I could hardly move except in the direction the water wanted. My friend grabbed my arm. I tried to bite him but we started floating back to the light. "I know what you're doing."

"Good," he said, "I don't know how much time we have."

He let go of the blanket, which became smaller and smaller. I could smell his boozy breath and his clothes drunk with sewer water. A half-filled yellow bottle with a woman on the label started to swim by. He scooped it up and tucked it inside his shirt. "She's mine," he said.

I thought I heard flapping overhead but I didn't have time to protect my head from all that evil. The water guided us to the dim light. We floated. There were signs and wonders along the way, a torn **entrance** sign, a painting of fruit, a child on a piece of wood crying. A man scissored his legs and scooped his arm into the gushing stream, a woman tried to do a jig while being carried away, a little squirrel knocked against the walls and then was swept away. I tried to concentrate. People and animals. The rats had already escaped, running up the stairs where my cart was waiting. My friend let go of my arm, splashed ahead of me, drinking from his new bottle. He waved and smiled with his missing teeth.

We were thrown forward. I saw that he had grabbed the stairs. Water went around them on its way to wherever it was going. I did the same thing. I was panting and I lay on a step for a while. Then I sat up and tried to catch a big brown bag full of clothes with a cigarette packet crowning the top. My clothes below my waist were a lumpy puddle.

I said, "That water is exceptionally devoted and has a mind of its own," to no one in particular.

I wiped the stairs with my pants and skirt and coat every time I moved. I was atmospheric and quivering. Something with blue fur whisked by. I started screaming, "The sky's a can opener."

A few stragglers were resting. A girl a few steps above me said, "Shut up you stupid bitch. We all nearly drowned. There's a lot of shit in that water."

A boy about the same age told her, "I bet they're just trying to get rid of us. This stupid-ass city's tired of runaways. It's easier to drown us all."

"I lost my shoes." The girl sounded like a magician. She was picking something off of her legs that looked like pieces of soggy tissue paper. "Maybe it's the beginning of something."

"Yeah," he said, "our invitation to leave."

By the time I pulled my weight slowly up the stairs my

friend was gone. I found his wet pants and socks. Where would he go without pants? Had he really been there? I hugged my cart. I hated being separated from my cart. I found my wriggling valuables and checked to be sure that they stood at attention. I closed my eyes. When I opened them I saw what the city would look like under water.

JIMMY, CHAPTER EIGHTEEN

I wanted to talk about Martine. The boy didn't like hearing about unbiblical romances he believed he'd never have. Emily didn't care much about dismantling the past, being more interested in the future. The guys at the diner had met Martine and would listen but it would remind them about relationships they may never have again.

THEM was now dispersing their meetings to different locations so they couldn't be found. I had to call up the office and give them a password I was given to find the nearest place and time. Sometimes it was someone's apartment or a spot in the park.

I stepped back underground. I was tired of being myself. I stood on the platform although I wasn't going anywhere that day. I bumped into a woman with a pink hat and an enormous black purse.

"Sorry," I said, "I'm on my way to my accountant. I'm a musician. My name's Gary." My hand was suspended in the trembling air. But she spun away, saying nothing, boarding a subway.

I sat on my usual bench. The people who came there each day would probably recognize me as a fixture.

A huge, hairless man at the bottom of the steps dropped his head into his hands and cried, "I have so many doubts. Mankind is falling apart." Then he balled up his newspaper and threw it on the ground. He stepped forward for a train and waited, saying to the man standing next to him, "Why not go to work? If the world's ending what else can we do?"

I picked up the newspaper and flattened it out. There was a front page article about rain pounding everywhere lately, dislodging plants, cascading from buildings, pooling everywhere. I noticed a group of black and white clad THEM missionaries grouped in a corner, nodding to one another like penguins agreeing. I heard the slurping sound of huge pumps nearby and I finally noticed sandbags decorating edges. The rain was fading and the subways seemed to be working fine. I didn't see what all the fuss was about. The newspapers had to make news.

"The power of suggestion," I was mumbling to myself, sitting in a dank corner. I tucked the newspaper under the bench.

"Once I was a little girl." The woman's words found me. I couldn't see her. The voice was familiar. "Now I'm exhausted."

"Who are you?" But then I suddenly knew.

"Kathleen." The ragged woman stared at me from behind a cement post. "I fought the water and the water didn't win."

She shook her head. She changed her disgusting gloves for another pair of disgusting gloves. A ring of dried soot circled the waist of her coat. "Did you catch that woman?"

"No, I guess she doesn't want to be caught."

"Not yet." She threw her head back and roared shamelessly, stupendously.

"I try to tidy up my own doubt but it runs faster and

catches up to me." I fiddled with the newspaper and she snatched it out of my hands, stuffed it into her cart. "I had a little boy once, named Phillip, and an almost-wife, called Martine. I wondered about the island they came from although I never got to see it." The homeless woman, whatever her name was, looked perplexed. "An island is a piece of land that's usually in a warm climate and surrounded by water..."

"I fought the water and the water won," she interrupted. Then she settled back down, sat on the bench, one hand on her cart.

"Martine had said, 'You need go there.'

"At that time I said, 'Why? Everyone I need is here.'

"I didn't go and I was sorry because when I held her dead body it still smelled exotic, of strange fruits and vegetables, and of the sun from that island." I wanted to tell someone.

"My father was a religious man. He was a principal. He tried not to show it. My mother had been a teacher at his school before they both died in a bicycle accident. They pedaled off a cliff in some rural area they were visiting while riding a two-seater bicycle. Apparently they hadn't seen the edge. When I was older I decided to work with reliable transportation.

"I imagined Martine's island with children running around barefoot, playing games. Adults were busy but they still enjoyed the children. The houses there weren't much since they only needed to repel sun and sand. All that water all around would confine me. If I went for a walk I'd eventually end up stymied, pushed aside by the ocean as though I was debris. I would be shipwrecked.

"Our bodies are so limited. They are their own islands. I could go there now but it wouldn't matter to anyone anymore. I would be reminded of Martine and my lack of her.

"After her death I didn't want to ask questions about my father's old religion, which was strict and punishing. That was when I began looking elsewhere. I believed Martine was with me the whole time in a way that my parents weren't. Maybe it was just guilt for possibly being a cause of her death. If she hadn't met me I wonder if she and Phillip would still be alive."

The homeless woman's gloves slapped together and I realized she was clapping. "I'm good at instructions." She looked around suspiciously. "Unless it's from crows."

"I've never wanted a woman so much. It's a good thing I didn't get her." I cupped my hand over my mouth, "That's a joke."

"Boo hoo," she said inappropriately. "I've seen her, you know."

"Who?"

"Martini."

"Where?"

"Flying around. She takes trains to West Woods. She's here, there, everywhere. If you wait a long time you'll see her."

She was frightening me. "What does she look like?"

"She has gray braids that she disguises. She's a wicked old hag." She stretched out her face, rolled her eyes. "She doesn't make good company. I scare her." She contorted her face again.

"Why?"

"Because I know what she and Brian are doing."

"What are they doing?"

"Using crows to make trouble."

Then she lost me. "That's Rosemary."

"Rosemary, Martini..." her hand flew into the air and pieces of her glove confettied off. "She must be the one half alive."

"The other woman is dead," I explained.

"How can you tell the difference?"

***

Emily batted her eyelashes and swept her hands into prayer position, against her cheek, "I think I'm in love."

I wasn't surprised. "Who's the lucky boy?" Emily was at that age.

Her hands dropped. "Aaron, of course."

But there was a jolt in my chest. We were sitting in her apartment because her mother went on a date with someone the night before and still hadn't returned. The inside of their apartment appeared to have housed a small hurricane. Clothes were scattered on the floor and draped on furniture. The contents of drawers seemed to be thrown on top of everything. Food was congealing in bowls and water was left in glasses. My apartment was pristine and empty in comparison. "Do you invite your friends here?"

"What friends?"

I wondered if the boy could hear us, if he could hear

this far away. "Why Aaron? And don't say he listens to you because my friends and I listen to you too."

"But I'm in love with you too." She flitted around the apartment, searching for something. She expertly avoided the piles of garbage masquerading as her and her mother's essentials. "Here," she lifted a pamphlet, "let's go to this." She handed it to me. At first I was reluctant to take it.

It was **Come Fly with Us**. Nothing religious.

She lifted her body up onto her toes. "I took ballet as a little girl." Her arms arched over her head. "I saw Rosemary, you know."

"When? And why didn't you tell me?" I was getting angry.

"If you don't calm down, I won't tell you." Her feet flattened out again. She grew smaller. "Aaron said you'd be mad if I didn't tell you right away, but I just glimpsed her leaving on the subway. There was nothing I could do. I'm pretty sure it was her, and it's not like I'd run after that woman. What do you see in her anyway?"

"A companion."

She looked at me askance. "You mean sex? Ugh, with that woman?"

"Now, now, now." I was tsking her. "No, it's more than that. It's hard to explain. There's an accumulated wisdom between us."

"Potential sex then." She nodded in understanding.

"So nothing has happened between you and Aaron?"

"Whatever do you mean, kind sir?" She batted her eyelashes again.

"You know exactly what I mean."

"No, of course not. Besides, I'd have to do everything." She sighed, placed a finger at her chin. "It's a thought though."

"Emily. Don't kid about this." I was too loud.

"I'm sorry. No, nothing has happened. Don't get all upset." She sat down and managed not to flatten an old Chinese food take-out container or sit on a plastic spoon. "But we do need to go to that acrobatics place and you can pretend to be the father or grandfather I've never had."

"Duly noted."

***

The diner was my reality. And that kindly emotion created its own world within the world. I needed to transfer whatever vestiges were left of that feeling elsewhere. Don, Jack, and Bill were straightforward, never hiding the truth, although it was, of course, tainted with their own experiences.

"I'm glad to see you're still alive," Bill said. He tossed the menu at the waitress who caught it mid-air.

"How are things going?" Don asked me. "The usual all around," he told the waitress, who was dressed in polka dots and an apron.

"I'm fine and nothing exciting has happened in my life lately, although I am searching for a person of interest." There was no longer any reason to keep secrets from them.

"That woman you were interested in?" Jack nodded knowingly.

"Yes, as a matter of fact." I thought of Emily. "But the woman's tied in with this religious group, and I don't know what's happening over there."

"I've been asking around about them," Don said, "and apparently there's a shake-up in leadership happening soon. What it's about isn't clear."

"They sound dangerous," Bill said.

"Isn't all religion dangerous?" Jack was laughing. "Women too."

"Yeah," Don laughed. "The spice of life."

"Watch your mouths," the waitress swung by with empty plates balanced in her hands and along her arm like a new style of sleeve. I noticed the tiny cross swinging between her breasts.

"Too bad you don't have a photograph of her."

"Or a police description."

I said, "Rosemary, or whatever her name is, has gray braids that she wears in different ways. She's close to my age."

"Nope, haven't seen anyone like that lately," Bill said and everyone nodded. "Wish we could help you out."

"I'll let you know if I see her," the waitress came by with our food, sliding it across the table expertly.

"This city is too big," Bill said.

"Yeah, so he's finally moving," Jack wagged his thumb at Bill.

"To a little place not too far away called West Woods. Have you ever heard of it?"

The name gave me a start. "I wasn't really sure it existed."

Bill laughed. "Yeah," he looked at his napkin, "I couldn't afford to go any further."

"How's our favorite girl doing?" the waitress yelled from across the room.

"You tell me," I told her.

"Well," Don said, "she did mention something about some circus classes she was promised by a certain someone."

"Yeah, yeah, yeah," I said. "I'll get to it."

"We could help you out since you're so busy with your entanglements," Bill offered.

"And I have been looking into it," Don looked at me slyly, "and we might be able to help you financially with them too."

I'd be off the hook. "Let me think about that." Emily might be mad.

"What's there to think about?" Jack said.

I was overwhelmed by their generosity. I picked up my egg salad sandwich. "Maybe we could actually eat." I tried not to sound mean. I watched the waitress do a little dance with glasses in her hands. Her polka dots flew everywhere.

"That's no fun here," Jack winked at the waitress.

***

I was trying to talk to Harold at the meeting. We waved hot cups of charred coffee at each other. This was a new secret meeting place that resembled the old one except that the chairs rustled, disputing each other, the tables were more stooped and sighing, and the windows looked out onto the street even more halfheartedly.

A young white girl with a pockmarked face sidled up to Harold. "So what's it like to be black?" She peered at her hands as though they might turn black at any moment.

Harold shuffled, looked at the floor, coffee spilling on the wooden floor.

"I'm a target all the time or else I'm erased and forgotten," Harold hesitated, thinking.

"Really?" the girl asked. "In this day and age?"

"Yeah," Harold said, "look around. How many black people are here to pin stuff on when things go wrong?"

I said, "What about that black guy that shot a white woman last month? There was a big uproar about race and then a week later, no one can even remember his name."

"Isn't that a little paranoid?" She looked at Harold and me.

"We blacks is scary." Harold made a vaudeville face. "Boo." The girl jumped back. "No, really," he said. "We have our own history and culture and some of it isn't very pretty."

"Yeah, but shouldn't people move on and not be isolated?"

"I'm not that different from you." Harold sipped more of the bitter-tasting coffee, then he put it aside. Harold dug in his pants pocket and pulled out a dime. "What color is this?"

"Silver," the girl said.

"And if it was a different color would it be worth something else? Like gold."

The girl blushed.

"But I can't dance and both of my parents were professionals. And I speak perfect English in case you didn't notice." Harold tried to define himself.

"I didn't really mean that," she was backing away from us.

"Now if you had to choose between two guys helping you move your furniture and one guy was white and another black, what would you do?"

The girl's pockmarked face fell, which was her answer. She mumbled some excuse and left, joining a group of boisterous girls.

"Now that we got rid of her, I wanted to ask you something," I told Harold, who was bravely refilling his coffee cup.

"No, I haven't heard anything more about Rosemary. That was her THEM name." Then he laughed. "I shor enoufs be scaring off that there girl."

"Ain't it a shame." We both laughed. "I wasn't going to ask you about Rosemary although I'm still looking for her."

"What were you going to ask me?"

"I'm trying to figure out what to do with the boy."

***

"I heard that you don't want to take care of the boy anymore." The woman was stunningly beautiful with long, blonde tresses that dangled over her shoulders. She was in her thirties. She looked like she was whispering to me from the cover of a fashion magazine. She wore a tight dress and bent over her large bag full of things for the boy. "I love being a mother and my kids are gone from home now. I could take the boy." She gave me a lovely smile as a gift. "Have you received everything from him that you need?"

"What are you talking about?"

"The boy's special in case you didn't notice," she searched her bag and retrieved a comb and began raking her hair.

I had thought the comb was for the boy. "I'm not sure."

She frowned and deep grooves formed over her perfect eyebrows. "You should know by now. I won't take him unless the process is complete."

"What process?"

"The process of give and take." She frowned, arranging articles in her enormous bag. "What is it that you think you want?"

I wondered what the boy could hear although when I looked in on him he appeared to be asleep. Appearances were always deceiving though.

Yesterday I had whispered to him, "You need to go somewhere else where people can concentrate on you more. I'm so distracted with everyone disappearing I can't take care of you or focus on anything." I had forgotten to complete certain of his hygienical procedures and there were consequences and more waste to clean up.

Emily is overwhelming.

As though he was reading my thoughts.

So you want me to disappear too?

If he had a voice, I might have detected the hurt in it or maybe not. "I think it's best for you to live with someone else."

I still believe in you. I might see or walk or speak or fly with your help.

I was cradling my head in my hands, "I was hoping for that too."

One blink. *Before I go??*

"I don't know what I want from him," I said to the beautiful woman who would be Aaron's new mother.

She smiled that smile again. "I think we project what we want onto Aaron since he's such a blank, clean slate."

"Maybe he's not so clean after living with me."

"I heard about all the mistakes," she said, lowering her lush eyelashes. "But minor infractions can be rectified."

"And, of course, he has needs. Plenty of them too," I added. I sat, "Tell me a little about you."

She sat down, crossed her hands on her knees, her posture impeccable. "My name's Dorothy..." she began.

I interrupted her. "Names don't matter with THEM."

She shook her head. "You're right. I'll just tell you a little bit about my circumstances. A few years ago my second husband ran off with a younger woman, who he used to work with. My kids are now all grown up and gone. I have a void. I have a large house and I love children. I want to take care of the boy."

"Have you cared for anyone disabled before?"

"Not really, except for my husband." She laughed a little and it was musical.

"How long have you been with THEM?"

"This feels like a job interview. Are you sure you want to give him up?"

"Yes, of course, you're right. It's really none of my business."

"I've been with THEM all my life. Even my parents belonged."

"You're a lifer?" I joked.

"Yes," she smiled, shyly. "My first husband was one of Brian's close associates. But the marriage didn't work out and he left THEM."

I wanted to ask what he had learned. "Why?"

"I can't discuss it. He died recently. But I'm still close to Brian."

I stood up and opened my front door. "I have to think about this some more."

"Don't I get to meet the boy?"

"Maybe next time." I held the door open for her, feeling one of my headaches beginning.

She gathered her large bag together. "I could help you bathe him right now." She moved toward the door.

"I'll let you know." I couldn't wait until she left.

Carly, Chapter Nineteen

My friend was slipping and sliding down the street toward me. As he got closer, I could see his beard full of debris, old food, wood chips, string, and something slimy. His hair was seaweed, his face was streaked with dirt, his pants fell off his backside, and his shoes were flopping around.

He was singing, "My bonnie lies over the ocean, my bonnie lies over the sea... bring back my bonnie to me." He fell once or twice. He held his bottle high so it wouldn't break.

"That water is a coat and it lives in the present," I screamed at him. He just looked at me. He started singing softly and trying to dance past me and my cart. "That water was living in my brain for a while, but now it's gone." He was past me, going down to the street corner with the blinking **Beer** sign. "Where'd you go?"

"To the depths of the bottom." He was trying to sing and laugh and not fall down.

I made a face at him, sink or swim. I was lonely and wanted something like a balloon that didn't pop or shake. I wrapped my arms around my cart and hugged.

He put his dirty hand on my cart. "You're a stupid door," I told him. My cart and I lurched backwards. His hand returned to his body.

"Now don't be that way, Betty." He was getting mad. "You got something I could use to get some money, don'cha now, me bonnie Betty?" He moved closer, showed me his mouth, where his teeth used to be.

He started to tickle me, but I bit him hard on the arm. "I know what you're doing."

He jumped away and waved his hurt arm around. "Fuck you."

"I'm your sister," I said, shaking my glove at him. He was unsteady. I blew on him and he fell back.

"I know you're hiding something. I don't know where it is." He scratched his beard.

Then I heard something like a fugue, too many cheerful voices telling me what to do. So I said, "Someone's arriving with too many implications."

A woman in loud heels was walking by. She was almost on top of me. "Calm down," she said to me, "here's a dollar. Get something to eat."

"It would take more than that," I screamed at her back.

My friend said, "Just shut the fuck up and take the money. If you don't want it, give it to me." He held out his hand.

I gave him the dollar. "Blood money," I said, a crow trying to nibble at my ear.

"You're alright." He pocketed the bill.

"I like the music."

"I'll show you where to sneak in, where there's music," he said.

My hands and mouth were working toward something. I could feel darkness coming. "I'm not sure what the crows would think."

"One took a potato chip right outta my hand once."

He was walking this way and that and my cart and I were following. "I hate feeling boiled," I added.

His hands were against a building and he was crumpling and then he stood up again. "I need to stop in here. You wait out here with your cart." He zigzagged inside the store that said **Liquor**. When he came out he was recognizable and smiling. We browsed by places I knew, the subway, marked streetlights, the parked car full of toy animals, the doorman who said hello, alleyways that coughed, the shrubs and doors that tried to grab me. My cart was always between us.

"You can't take that cart where we're going," his back warned me.

But I held on tighter. "Even your mouth can't rudder you."

His hands flew up into the air. "I'm just telling you." He took a gulp from his bottle. "We're almost there."

There was some grass and not-quite trees trying to grow near some benches. We were near the park. The sky was inevitable. There was a big tent embracing something. When my friend was busy with his bottle, I hid my cart behind some bushes that were digging deep into the ground nearby that seemed to be behaving. Something else, tall and bright, turned round and round with fake horses trying to get out of each other's way. Children were screaming and overran the place. "I'm nostalgic," I said.

"That's not all you are." He pointed at the tent. Then I heard it, a small, harmless song coming from inside. "Like I told you, you can't bring the cart inside." He glanced in my cart's direction. He lifted up part of the tent between two sticks. "It's warmer in there than you'd think, and you can dig out some popcorn and candy from the bleachers sometimes. You gotta be real quiet." He held out his hand, "So gimme my present."

I spat at him, patted my ghost-maker, and slipped underneath, toward the music.

"Don't say I never done nothing for you, bitch. You'll give it to me sooner or later. I know you got it." He scratched his beard. "Fuck, if only I could remember what it was."

Inside I could hardly hear him cursing outside. The music swirled around the room, looking for someone. The cursing fell down, moved away. I lay down like he had told me between the seats. I could see the floor salted with dust, footprints, chewed plastic toys, old paper cups, popcorn, candy wrappers with half-eaten candy, napkins, peanuts, and little yellow flags for the children. I ate some, picking through everything. The music was working its way around the room. Suddenly, bees swarmed beneath the melody and I started swatting them over my head. A gust began and Things started dropping out of the sky, trying to catch one another. I hid deeper under the seats. I cowered, whispering over and over again, "I know what they're trying to do."

Jimmy, Chapter Twenty

Emily was reading a pamphlet on the stairway between our two apartments and my heart skipped when I saw her. On closer inspection I saw that it was about acrobatics. When my heart quieted down, I could hear someone playing classical music upstairs, someone else moving furniture, and a neighbor downstairs fighting with someone. The stairwell echoed. I could hear almost everything. I got used to it and my hearing wasn't what it used to be. I stood a few steps below her.

"Fooled you," she said, wearing a smock draped over one shoulder and pants that formed bowls at their bottoms, "I bet you believed that you converted me." She had some kind of a striped bow in her hair.

I raised my hands high into the air and allowed them to drift down as I shook them. "Yes, I must be the Messiah." Then I sat down. "With a bum heart."

"Have you had your heart looked at?"

"Not really. Or my arms and legs and other parts."

"What's the matter with them?" She put the pamphlet aside, looked at me.

"I don't know. Nothing works as well as it used to."

"Don't you get medical benefits?"

"Some," I confessed to Emily, the practical one. "There's probably a part of me that doesn't want to know what's wrong."

"No wonder they gave you Aaron. No wonder you can't find that old crabapple Rosemary." She picked up her pamphlet again. "But then my grandfather went to the doctor all the time and he died of an aneurysm. So what good did that do him?"

"Life shouldn't be such a big mystery, where I don't know what happens to someone I care about. And it shouldn't be a fable where people represent something other than what they are," I told Emily. "It needs to be more real." We were arguing with ourselves, not each other. I fumbled with my hands. "I'm trying to give Aaron away right now."

Emily looked horrified, as though I had slapped her. "Why?"

"I'm in transition and I can't take care of him."

"What kind of transition?"

"I've seen enough in the transportation industry to know that I'll be moving on soon." I could tell Emily anything.

"I could help you take care of Aaron. And where are you going?"

"He needs new clothes all the time since he's growing. The helpers bring some, but he needs bed pans changed, baths, food, hair cutting, nails cut. More than I can tell you. And I don't know where I'm going."

"You need to be more specific. We can talk about this later."

"I met a woman who wants to take Aaron but I didn't like her."

"Who are you looking for?"

"I don't know yet."

"I was going to invite you to my acrobatic swinging display but now I'm not so sure I want to." She swung her arms around like a monkey.

"I didn't even know you'd had lessons."

She smiled. "You don't know much do you?"

***

"I don't know what I want," I confessed to Jack and Don at the diner. Bill was absent. He was moving into his new house. No one had seen it yet. I watched pigeons sweeping by the window above cars as though they were trying to keep pace with them. I moved the utensils around our table because my hands needed something to do. I wasn't really hungry.

"You know people come and go in our lives," Don was trying to be helpful.

"Mostly they go." I was quiet for a moment. "I'm not trying to sound bitter."

Jack said, "It comes with the territory."

"You mean about the boy?" Don shrugged as he sipped some coffee with a coil of steam above its surface.

I was silent for a moment. We hadn't talked about Aaron although he was implied since Emily had joined our group of old men and, I assumed, told them everything. They had been waiting for me to broach the subject. There was still more I should do for him. The same was true for Emily. Neither of them was my child. They were probably better off elsewhere. "It's complicated." The only person still living with me was the one I wasn't sure I wanted. A truck rattled our window and light jangled our forks and knives. I stared at everything except Jack's and Don's faces.

"It's a big responsibility," Don stated. "Emily didn't say much except that he's smart and limited and that it all has something to do with that religious group. But she likes him."

"Yes." I didn't want to elaborate, but then I said, "He has problems with his eyes and legs and he's mute."

"I can hardly take care of myself," Jack said, smiling, "which you already know."

They were trying to be understanding. "Thanks." I patted their age dappled hands without thinking. Jack withdrew his. It wasn't one of our usual gestures.

"You're getting soft, Jimmy," Jack said without looking at me.

"What's wrong with that?" Don inquired.

"I guess its fine as long as nobody shoots you." Jack was fidgeting with his empty plate.

"Can a leopard change its spots?" Don asked rhetorically.

"If its spots aren't too different," Jack was mumbling. "We're all disabled in some way. Right?" He wasn't really asking anyone. He continued, "What if the boy was whole?" It was almost an afterthought.

The waitress came by, her too-blonde hair dangling in her face. She wore a dress that acted busy, like a puzzle, with geometric pieces. A white apron held it down.

"I'm moving on," I told her.

"We're not going to see you here anymore?" she asked, frowning, her order pad balled up in her fist at her hip.

"I don't know." I shook my head. "I'm still not sure what I'm doing."

"These guys would be lost without you, with Bill moving and everything." She looked at Jack and Don. "And that talented sweet Emily. She did a few cartwheels when nobody was here and balanced on one of those stools, even as it twirled around. She's getting damned good. I can't wait to see her show."

"Neither can I," I said.

"It's tomorrow. We're all meeting here. Bill's coming back from West Woods. Do you want to go with us?" Someone yelled for her and she swirled around, her dress flaring.

"Thanks. But I have so much to do, taking the boy and everything." I had just that minute decided.

"See you there," and she hurried to her customer.

***

"I'll miss you," I told the boy.

I'm still here.

"Everyone I care about ends up missing."

One blink.

"Maybe after they're gone I realize that I care for them."

What's the difference?

"It's hard to pay attention to your life. Is one thing following or related to another?" All my soft parts were showing and I needed to stuff them back inside.

Keep me. Maybe your friends can help.

"You've been talking to Emily again."

One blink.

"I don't think they have that much money and I really couldn't ask them. I think we should go to Emily's acrobatic show tonight. We'll surprise her. What do you think?"

Aaron began shivering with excitement. I hadn't seen him like that. His eyes fluttered in his sockets. His arms and legs shook the bed. His torso flapped a bit. His head darted on his pillow. Wetness sprang from his eyes.

***

Emily was a whirlwind descending the stairs. She was carrying a sequined costume in a bag. Feathers sprouted out of the zippered top. She romped down the stairs three at a time. She was shoeless. She was flying. I imagined a city of acrobats, with everyone airborne, leaping everywhere, no doors, everyone hurtling in and out of windows, no need for streets, only wires across buildings. One of her hands lightly gripped the staircase rail.

"There she is. The Wonderful Emily, acrobat extraordinaire."

"Shush," she said, stopping. "My mother doesn't know anything about the lessons or the show."

"What did she think about your outfit?"

"She thinks it's for some school prom." Emily laughed. "As if I'd wear something like that to a dance, even if I was in school."

"Aaron and I are coming to your show tonight, and I wondered if you'd like to help me get him ready. You could see all the work it takes to get him out and you could assist me."

"I can't," she said. "I have to rehearse my naturally limber body now." She lifted one leg close toward her head. "Besides, I have a new boyfriend, didn't I tell you? His name is Nathan but we call him Nail for short. Anyway, I'll see you guys tonight. The whole crew from the diner should be there." She flipped her shiny outfit to her other arm, and it rustled like a caged bird. She kissed me on the cheek. "I'm so glad you both are coming."

"Break a leg." I kissed her cheek, thinking that sometimes all we needed was understanding.

"Maybe I shouldn't have invited you after all."

***

I could hear Brian's voice issuing from the television but I didn't want to upset the boy as I got him ready to go out. I turned the sound lower. I knew the boy could hear. Aaron was oddly quiet and subdued after his initial excitement, and I didn't want to disturb him further. He did everything I asked of him without complaints or fear or the usual questions, as if he had done this many times before. In his bath he cleaned everywhere without a murmur or argument. I dried him, brushed his hair, clothed him, fed him. I cut his nails, trimmed his hair, and sat him in his portable wheelchair with sunglasses. He hardly moved unless he had to.

Brian was answering questions, "Yes, changes are coming." He pointed at a newscaster, "And no, I can't tell you what they are yet." Brian looked like Brian for the interview, but he said he used disguises when he needed to, out in public. "Yes, I'm worried about attempts on my life and my mother's." "Yes, THEM is considering buying the town of West Woods for a variety of reasons. We do believe there is a spiritual confluence in that geographical area. It would also be a place we wouldn't be disturbed." He pointed at a newswoman. But I couldn't hear the question. The reply was, "Loss is difficult and maybe that's where everything exists."

"Belonging," I told the boy, "is a relative term."

Aaron moved slowly around in his wheelchair and finally he wrote, *Maybe they just need another leader.*

The newswoman continued, "Since that interview Brian Aimsworth and his mother have disappeared. There is speculation that they might have absconded with at least some of the organization's funds or gone underground for their safety. They could be disguised and among us right now. But we do know that no additional bodies have been found."

It was as if the boy already knew. I thought about Rosemary. And then I wondered who would take Brian's place? Aaron? Harold? The guy with the ponytail? Or someone else, someone we didn't know yet?

The boy and I swiveled our heads towards one another. We stared at each other, if you could call it that.

***

The boy and I settled into good seats inside the circus tent at the periphery of the park. Aaron had a front aisle seat and we folded the wheelchair in back of our section. I sat right in back of him, so I could watch him and what was going on, and I could whisper a description of the events if necessary. We were seven rows back, but I could see well. Children threw popcorn at each other and spilled drinks before the show began. Bill, Don, Jack, and the waitress sat a few rows away us, in another section, but close to us. They held signs, encouraging Emily.

The show began with elephants stomping around the ring and girls somersaulting on their rough, gray backs like beautiful, glittering fleas. A lion tamer in a cage snapped a whip at two lions. A middle-aged man with a red beard and mustache and a cap with a brim over his red hair sat down late near us, in the middle of the row. He tucked in his coat and looked around and then stared at the ring, pulling out a bottle from his pocket. There was something oddly familiar about him although he was one of those men on the fringe of life that I could have seen in the city. His clothes seemed to have had lots of experiences. Aaron and I watched the three ring circus which would soon feature acrobats-in-training from the nearby school. Lions leaped through rings of fire and clowns danced about, squeezing their large, red noses and the noses of children within touching distance. Aaron was interested but quiet, not excited at all, which surprised me. I whispered descriptions to him. He wrote that he'd never been to a circus before.

"There's a clown who looks like my friend Bill on the stage. He has flat, white hair, weird eyeglasses, a red mouth, and white face and he's playing a trumpet and pacing in his enormous shoes." I was at that age when everyone reminded me of everyone else. And I knew that every act, in some way, was an illusion.

I can hear children and smell sugar. His nose sniffed the air.

I thought I saw the homeless woman, Patty or Natasha or whatever her name was. She scurried back and forth along the aisles, her rags flapping as if she was looking for something. Someone stopped her and asked her what she was doing.

"I paid the yellow birds like everybody else." She wagged a finger at the man. "I won't let them get away with it." She cupped her fingers over her mouth.

I thought about going over to help her, but she was gone. "Now there's so much action and all different colors under the bright lights. The spotlights are on monkeys riding horses in a tiny ring and jugglers throwing pins in the air." I looked at the boy's face. "Are you enjoying this or is there not enough besides the music to hear?"

Where's Emily?

"I think all the students are coming up soon. Hold on." I patted his back.

Shortly Emily did come onstage. She was with three other students, and she looked wonderful, shining, with all those feathers. They all threw their arms over their heads before they proceeded climbing the swings. Emily was thin and adolescent and her blue eyes shone. There were two boys, maybe one was Nail, and another girl. They swung through the air, mostly on trapezes, grabbing one another's arms or legs and spinning or twirling or somersaulting in the nothingness until they grabbed someone or landed somewhere. She was amazingly graceful and sinewy. She would be a lovely woman. All the students were good and the music highlighted their stunts. No one was watching the fire-eater or the leopards and tigers jumping through hoops of fire in the other two rings. Everybody's heads were raised. There was a net below the acrobats in the third ring. Thank God, I thought.

"Emily's on right now," I told Aaron, "with the three other students. They're dancing in the air as long as they can before they have to grab onto something solid. It's like they're made of air. They're all great."

I know. I can tell.

The boy's head swiveled to the back where there was some kind of a commotion. How could he tell how good Emily was? Maybe it was the crowd's excitement or the music or the sound of bodies pedaling and turning, flesh against flesh. There was a fight behind us that grew louder, but all I wanted to do was watch Emily. I didn't want to be disturbed, but I looked back.

What's going on?

Natasha was scuffling with a man. She punched the man, who was trying to hold her down, and she bent down, and when she stood up, she was holding a gun and pointing it all around the audience and then at the man she'd been fighting with. The man ran away and hid somewhere.

So she pointed it back in our direction and said, "I know what you're doing. I've known all along."

Then she fired at the man with red hair who sat near us. The noise was deafening and close, even with the music from the stage. He ducked under his seat. I couldn't tell whether he was hurt or not. She kept on firing as though she didn't know how to stop. It didn't seem real until everyone panicked and began running for the doors. I didn't know how to save the boy from being crushed by people rushing in front of us. I needed to get him to his wheelchair. The cats in the ring went wild and knocked over the fire hoops and the tent caught on fire. I saw flames spreading out in lines like children's drawings of the sun before Natasha shot me through the throat and then my legs collapsed. I reached for Aaron but he was already gone.

***

I was alive. I could tell I was in the hospital by the antiseptic smell and other medical odors, the sound of machines, doors, soft-soled shoes, conversations, the feel of the bed with bars, tubes in and out, the sheets. Everything had happened so fast. My eyes were bandaged with cottony squares, my legs were in stiff casts and suspended, and I couldn't move them. There was something wrong with my neck and I had trouble swallowing. I licked my lips and I noticed that I had a tongue. My ears, nose, and mouth seemed intact.

When I moved my hand to check everything on my

body again, a familiar female voice said, "So you're finally awake. Don't remove anything or they'll have to strap your hands down. I'll give you a pad and paper. You'll have to learn to use them without using your eyes."

Who are you? I tried to write, but I didn't know what it looked like on the page. I thought of how good the boy had become at writing. I didn't think it was Emily's voice. And then I knew who it was.

"You know me as Rosemary but my real name is Alexis Bell."

She hesitated and then ran her warm hand over my hair, kissed my cheek. I thought I could feel her gray braids thump the sheet and blanket over my chest as she leaned down. I wanted to take her in my arms but I couldn't, not yet. Every part hurt. I could smell her perspiration.

"I'll try and explain what I know. Someone, they think it was a homeless woman, tried to shoot a lot of people and it set off a panic and a fire onstage. A man finally knocked her down and got the gun. But the fire spread quickly, killing about fifteen people. Most of the animals escaped. Emily and her friends are fine. She's been here to see you while you've been out the last few days. She'll be back." She sniffled a little. "Aaron is here. He was brought to the hospital by your friends, Bill, Jack, and Don, who also saved you." She hesitated. "The authorities haven't found the homeless woman who started the whole thing, but she could be burned and still unidentified. It was a huge fire. At least they stopped it just before it spread into the park."

I scribbled *Brian is missing?*

"Yes, he is."

Do you think Brian will ever come back?

"I hope not."

Why did you leave me?

"It was what I needed to do then but now it's different."

How do I know that you'll stay now?

"You don't know. But right now we need to discuss your injuries. Jimmy, the doctors think that you'll be blind because of the smoke from the fire and your larynx has been damaged so much by a bullet that they don't think you will be able to use your voice. Your legs were hit and the lower part of your femurs were shattered by either one bullet that went straight through both your legs or two separate bullets. They weren't sure. So the doctors aren't sure about you ever walking again."

I resembled the boy.

"I'll be with you as long as you need me. And I like taking care of people," Alexis, or Rosemary, took my inquisitive hand into hers and patted it. "This is all about you. It was always about you, not the boy."

It was all too much. I heard a door nearby swing open and footsteps hurried to my bed followed by several others. Air from a corridor rushed inside the room. It was full of food smells and perfume and ointments. Metal trays clanged. I could hear several conversations down the hallway. I tried to move my arms and legs and the little I could of my injured head.

"Jimmy, Jimmy, Jimmy," Emily cried as she ran to hug me where she could, where there weren't any tubes or bandages. "I'm so glad you're okay. Bill, Jack, and Don are here too. It's all so terrible what happened. I feel horrible for inviting everybody." She turned toward someone. "He knows I'm here, right? His arms are moving."

A female voice said, "I'm sure he does, and he's very happy, but right now I need to sedate him. His heart can't take much more. He needs to calm down. You can come and see him later."

"No, no," I wanted to say but nothing came out. I couldn't even blink. My hands spun, hitting soft objects. So this is what it will be like, I thought, before something warm and flowing filled me to the brim.

***

In the hospital, when the voices didn't drift in and out, I inhabited a city of my own memories, ideas, alternatives as I lay still, recovering. Everything hurt more than before. Time spread out a blanket, got comfortable. Martine and Phillip, along with everyone else I'd known, visited in one form or another. So many thoughts came and went, a complex train system not controlled by my mind. At first I wondered what I could have done differently, not attending Emily's show, or not bringing Aaron, not involving Bill, Jack, or Don. Was fate unavoidable? Would our outcomes have been the same no matter what I did? My heart couldn't withstand several operations. I was old. Had my own story become too large for my body? Bill, Jack, and Don visited.

I was too handsome to kill.

"Ha, ha," Jack said.

"Too cranky," Don decided.

"The waitress from the diner gave me a card for you. It has a sad puppy on the front and inside it says, 'Take your drugs or else I will.'" Bill placed the card on the table near my shoulder. "And here's one from Emily, handmade, with a mess of blue colors on the front. Inside it says, 'Too bad you can't see this beautiful card I made for you but we'll always have the beach, old man.'"

"Hell," Jack declared, "I'm not going to ask about that."

Thanks for saving us.

"Yeah," Don said, "it was smoky but we all worked fast. And Aaron's doing really good here."

"Hey, Buddy, the nurses are looking mean and visiting hours are over. Is there anything we can do for you or get you?" Jack laughed.

Everything.

* * *

Now I'm like you. An orderly had wheeled the boy into my room, announcing, "Aaron is here," although I could already sense him. Emily, who continued to visit, entered and sat between his wheelchair and my bed. My memories spasmed which felt like pain in my head.

"I'm going to read your notes to each other out loud and try not to add my own comments," Emily claimed.

No, not like me. Doctors believe they can repair my legs or give me new ones and, maybe, fix my eyes. I will always be mute. What about you?

I'm old, beyond repair. Emily stamped her feet at that. But she didn't say anything more than what I'd written.

Good circus until…

Everything's waiting to burn or is full of regret. What will you do now?

I'll be like you. No more watching other people's lives pass before me. I'll have my own, go to school, cry, laugh, love, hate, smoke cigarettes behind a dumpster, do what I can.

I could feel Emily smiling as she read Aaron's note.

And THEM? I wrote.

They want someone to make something happen for them. They never really wanted ME. His pencil stopped scratching for a moment. *What will you do?*

Don't know. Maybe it's time to let someone take care of me, which can be penance or love, or something in between.

CARLY, CHAPTER TWENTY ONE

"Everything's outside my body," I screamed in the subway station. "Everything that's supposed to be inside my body is outside." I checked for blood. I held up an orange, my heart. Inside my cart I found my bones, TV antennae that I raised up to my spine. I patted my wire ribs, holding everything together. My muscles, wheels, my tongue, a ping pong paddle . One lung, a hot water bottle. I didn't know how to get them back inside. I lifted the gun that was my mouth to say something in their direction and the Things yelled and ran away again.

"Empty," I explained loudly and tossed the ghost-maker into my cart. It couldn't complain anymore, underneath everything else that was my body. My friend would be mad but I didn't care. Then I hid behind the stairs, away from the eerie light, so the crows could tell me what to do next.

***

Two days ago I had seen my friend spinning around the street with his new bottle, his beard resting over his shoulder, a kind of human moss. He told me that the police were rounding up all the women without homes because the big tent in the park burned down.

"Shit," he said careening into a streetlamp and hitting his ear, "some bad shit went on in there. Did you see it all?

Man," he said, "you're lucky you got out. Lots of people burned to a crisp and everything." He laughed, his teeth showing like open windows. "If I was you, I'd make sure the cops don't find me until it all blows over." He scratched his chin through all that vegetation. "Hey man, wasn't there something I wanted from you? Fuck if I can remember what the hell it was." He smiled, raising his eye windows. "If I hear of a good place to stay I'll let you know." He poked one finger from around his bottle at me and then he wandered off.

I misled myself to the grocery store parking lot where doors opened and closed by themselves. Things picked out their own special carts, used them, and then abandoned them. Grass was where it wasn't supposed to be. Litter I couldn't use tucked itself behind car tires. The gravel hurt my feet. I had to swat at crows constantly and talk to them. Otherwise, they kept on dive-bombing me.

"Motherfuckers," I shouted.

A miniature Thing with blue eyes behind glass orbits that fried people's eyes pulled on her mother's dress hem, said, "What's the matter with that lady over there?" She pointed her finger at me like a gun.

The mother, her arms full of food trying to claw its way out of her paper bags, said, "Don't mind her. She's a crazy woman. Don't even look at her, Sweetie. Just get inside the car." She opened the back of her car and locked the escaping edibles inside. She opened the front door, her windshield busy reflecting me.

"But she has something shiny in her hand, Mommy." She retracted her accusing finger.

"Shit," the mother said, dunking with the little Thing along the side of their car and creeping inside.

I walked up to them as the car engine kept on screeching to turn on again and again. I tapped the ghost-maker against their shut window, said, "Can you give me something to stop all these crows?"

"Here," the mother yelled and tossed her wallet out the window just as the car started and ran off with them.

I put my ghost-maker back under my clothes and took the plastic colored cards from the wallet and planted them in the dirt near the parking lot so they could grow into something to eat. I kept the money for later. I could use it to make a different kind of fire than the one that tried to lick me under the big tent. I started to play a game of cards with all her photographs when I heard screaming cars coming this way. I grabbed my cart and left. I could hear policemen arriving, the noise disappearing, replaced with talking and more talking and footsteps all around the area. But it was fading behind me.

I went where no one would notice me, where I could hide, The Women's Shelter. It was hell. I hated it there. A woman cackled over dinner, swooping her arms around the mashed potatoes and stringy turkey that was turning a terrible blue, like a sick sky. I thought about the food digested outside of me. I missed my cart, camouflaged for the night outside, near the children's playground, by some Jungle Gyms and swings.

"My feet are plotting against me."

Someone picked imaginary lice out of my hair and I bit

their arm. A man was lecturing us. I spit when I thought of Brian but the man couldn't get into my brain. He didn't have the right words. There were so many women like me that I fit right in. It smelled badly, and we couldn't open any windows. Cabbage, sweat, bird shit, the foul stuff from mouths and all the body could offer. Some of the women were loud and angry, others tucked themselves into boxes and corners. One woman tried to jump from chair to chair and someone that wasn't me knocked her down.

"Vagina," someone yelled.

"Penis," someone answered. "That shit always gets you into trouble."

We were all locked in for the night.

All their talk kept the voices of the crows away.

"Hey, you," the woman with torn blonde hair and a jangling vest in the bed next to mine said to my sometimes face, "shut up your muttering, or I'll get you thrown out of here." She pulled at her hair.

"Fucking bitch," another woman said, digging her face into her pillow.

I couldn't sleep with all those soft bodies surrounding mine, the snoring, blistery dreams that rose up out of the women and popped against the walls and doors leaving a sticky collar of time around my neck. I tried sleeping underneath the bed but returned to its soft roof. There was a burning from the ghost-maker tucked near my chest and then a scary click from it. But it was empty. I turned on my side and fixed it under the measly covers. I wasn't afraid with it.

My feet fell asleep in an adult way. Suddenly a noisy door burst open and Dead Things in blue uniforms rushed in, jostling the females awake, nudging us, clapping, looking at our faces with a shiny tunnel of light, searching the innermost rooms of our bodies and minds. I scrambled under the bed. Some made it out the door.

The blonde woman next to me told them, "I know who you're looking for. She's right over there. The one with a gun who did something terrible." I could see a little bit of her.

I couldn't see who she was pointing at. I shuddered, staring at the convulsive box springs. The blonde woman was decomposing. She began tearing out her hair again.

Another woman was dragged out, pulling against handcuffs, kicking at the men's pants. "Bastards," she screamed. "I was married to all of you."

I slipped outside right after them, before the shelter woke everyone else up to begin the day. Night welcomed me with a brief moon and stars that moaned and tried to accumulate under my fingernails, so I could take them with me. When I cleared off the bushes and branches, I hugged my cart, sighed, shared my story without looking back.

***

Before I left my cart at the subway station, I kissed it all over and then I stepped onto the train heading for West Woods, where I could fall asleep. From the too bright window I saw them wheeling the new Dis that took Brian's place. I spit his name. Jimmy. The Dis looked like a crow, black suit, feathers where his hair used to be. I wasn't sure about him or his transformation. Who was he supposed to be now? And that Martini was with him, the one that used to follow Brian around. She had gray braids. I spit again. I hoped the old man was happy. Those Things in black and white weren't in the subways anymore. There were changes. Sometimes that young Thing was with them, her eyes another shade of blue. Once I saw her do a cartwheel in her short red dress when the station wasn't so full. Yesterday I saw a few Things, along with Martini, bend down and ask the old Dis something and I saw him blinking once over and over again as if he was a traffic light and we were all his traffic. That was right after a circle of blinding light suddenly kissed my face.

LAURIE BLAUNER is the author of four previous novels, eight books of poetry, and a forthcoming creative non-fiction book. She won PANK's 2020 Creative Non-fiction Book Contest and her book, called *I Was One of My Memories,* will be available in 2021. Her latest novel, titled *The Solace of Monsters*, won the 2015 Leapfrog Fiction Contest, was listed in Book Riot's "A Great Big Guide to Wonderful Books of 2016 from Indie Presses," and was a 2017 Washington State Book award finalist in Fiction. Her three other novels were published by Black Heron Press. Her most recent book of poetry, *A Theory for What Just Happened*, is available from FutureCycle Press. She has received an NEA Fellowship as well as Seattle Arts Commission, King County Arts Commission, 4Culture, and Artist Trust grants and awards. Her work has appeared in *The New Republic, The Nation, The Georgia Review, American Poetry Review, Mississippi Review, Field, Caketrain, Denver Quarterly, The Colorado Review, The Collagist, The Best Small Fictions 2016* and many other magazines. She lives in Seattle, Washington. Her web site is laurieblauner.com.